"WHAT DID THEY DO TO YOU?"

Buffy opened the coffin lid and picked up the body of Brian Andrews. As she examined it, she asked it questions, not expecting answers. "Did you really drown, or was it something else?"

What she saw next made her nearly drop the body onto the floor. Through the dead, open eyes, Buffy could see faint light. She turned the body so it was directly in front of the lamp on the small table. It seemed unbelievable, but it was true. Light from the lamp was visible through the lifeless orbs of Brian Andrews's eyes, like light glowing through a nightmarish jack-o'-lantern. The lamplight was shining through Brian's head an̶ ̶n̶o̶t̶ ̶h̶i̶s̶ eyes.

Because ther̶ ̶ ̶ ̶ ̶ ̶ ̶ ̶ ̶ ̶ ̶ ̶k the light but a little bo̶

Br̶

Buffy the Vampire Slayer™

Buffy the Vampire Slayer
  (movie tie-in)
The Harvest
Halloween Rain
Coyote Moon
Night of the Living Rerun
Blooded
Visitors
Unnatural Selection
The Power of Persuasion
Deep Water
Here Be Monsters
Ghoul Trouble
Doomsday Deck
The Angel Chronicles, Vol. 1

The Angel Chronicles, Vol. 2
The Angel Chronicles, Vol. 3
The Xander Years, Vol. 1
The Xander Years, Vol. 2
The Willow Files, Vol. 1
The Willow Files, Vol. 2
How I Survived My Summer Vacation,
  Vol. 1
The Faith Trials, Vol. 1
Tales of the Slayer, Vol. 1

The Lost Slayer serial novel
  Part 1: Prophecies
  Part 2: Dark Times
  Part 3: King of the Dead
  Part 4: Original Sins

Buffy the Vampire Slayer adult books

Child of the Hunt
Return to Chaos
The Gatekeeper Trilogy
  Book 1: Out of the Madhouse
  Book 2: Ghost Roads
  Book 3: Sons of Entropy
Obsidian Fate
Immortal
Sins of the Father

Resurrecting Ravana
Prime Evil
The Evil That Men Do
Paleo
Spike and Dru: Pretty Maids
  All in a Row
Revenant
The Book of Fours
The Unseen Trilogy (Buffy/Angel)
  Book 1: The Burning
  Book 2: Door to Alternity
  Book 3: Long Way Home

The Watcher's Guide, Vol. 1: The Official Companion to the Hit Show
The Watcher's Guide, Vol. 2: The Official Companion to the Hit Show
The Postcards
The Essential Angel
The Sunnydale High Yearbook
Pop Quiz: Buffy the Vampire Slayer
The Monster Book
The Script Book, Season One, Vol. 1
The Script Book, Season One, Vol. 2
The Script Book, Season Two, Vol. 1
The Script Book, Season Two, Vol. 2

Available from SIMON PULSE

Buffy the Vampire Slayer™

POWER OF PERSUASION

Elizabeth Massie

A novelization by Elizabeth Massie.
Based on the hit TV series created by Joss Whedon

SIMON PULSE

New York London Toronto Sydney Singapore

This book is a work of fiction. Any references to historical events, real people, or real locales are used fictitiously. Other names, characters, places, and incidents are the product of the author's imagination and any resemblance to actual events or locales or persons, living or dead, is entirely coincidental.

First Simon Pulse edition October 2002
First Pocket Books edition October 1999

SIMON PULSE
An imprint of Simon & Schuster
Children's Publishing Division
1230 Avenue of the Americas
New York, NY 10020

The text of this book was set in Times.
Printed in USA

10 9 8 7 6 5 4

ISBN: 0-671-02632-1

This is dedicated to some very cool people in my life:

Erin, Brian, and Ben—for being young, bright, talented, wacky, compassionate, hopeful, and all things that are good. I love you!

Yvonne Navarro—for being a great friend and inspiration for many years, no matter how far away you are!

Lisa Clancy—How cool can an editor be, anyway?? Thanks for everything!

PROLOGUE

The blood-covered cleaver hovered in the air, tossing off red-tinted light, and then slammed down, slicing through the thick flesh and clear to the wood beneath it. The cleaver was then twisted, pulled loose, and lifted high again. A moment's pause and it was driven downward and into the flesh once more. All across the floor and walls, bits of skin, blood, and bone lay like gruesome leaves scattered to the wind. The cleaver was tugged free. The man wiped sweat from his brow with the back of a sausage-fat hand, gritted his teeth, then forced the blade down again in a whistling arc.

"Dad," said the tall, plain, brown-haired girl standing by the refrigerator with her arms crossed. "It would have been a whole lot easier to buy chicken already cut up. You're making an incredible mess."

"I'm doing fine," said Mr. Gianakous as the cleaver went down again, severing a chicken wing and sending the outer piece skittering across the counter. All around the shiny new kitchen of the soon-to-open restaurant lay evidence of Mr. Gianakous's lack of cooking ability—

the chicken bits, a pan of burned wine sauce, a lumpy ball of dough that was supposed to become some sort of Greek bread.

"But you aren't exactly doing fine," said Allison Gianakous. "Maybe we should hire a cook? Please?"

"Oh, but I *can* cook!" said Mr. Gianakous. He turned and gave his daughter one of his patronizing grins. He was a balding man with a black mustache and a double chin. Just over a month ago he had been an insurance salesman. Now, he was proprietor and chef of the first official Greek restaurant in Sunnydale, California. "I was told in my dream that this is my true calling. The Laughing Greek is going to be one fantastic restaurant, my girl. Don't worry your pretty little head about a thing."

Allison gritted her teeth. "Dad, I'm not pretty and I'm not little. I wish you wouldn't say that."

Mr. Gianakous wiggled his eyebrows. "I inherited my culinary talent from my Greek ancestors," he said. He slammed the blade into the chicken, rending the spine with a pulpy snap. "And you get your beauty from your mother, God rest her soul."

"What if we hire somebody who has, well, more experience?" asked Allison. "Just to help out at first? Or we could get Alex to come over after his classes at Crestwood. He actually makes some pretty decent eggplant dip and—"

Mr. Gianakous tipped his face in Allison's direction, and by the tight expression he wore she knew she had stepped over the line. Radello Gianakous was not an abusive father, but he was very controlling, and Allison had never in all her sixteen years felt strong enough to challenge him.

"Alexander needs his free time," her father said sternly. "He's a college man now, and college men need to run a little wild, have some fun, impress the girls. That is as important to a man's education as hours spent hunched over a pile of books."

"But, Dad—"

"No buts." Mr. Gianakous smiled suddenly and ruffled Allison's hair with his sticky, chickeny fingers. "You're a good helper. We'll make The Laughing Greek a restaurant that Sunnydale will never forget."

"Oh," said Allison. "You can bet on that. Never forgotten." And under her breath, "Never lived down."

Mr. Gianakous turned his attention back to the job at hand. He whacked the chicken a few more times, then crammed the pieces into a baking pan. He fingered the knob on the industrial-sized stove to somewhere between 500 and 510 degrees, never once looking at a cookbook to see what temperature it needed or how long it should cook.

Allison muttered, "I'll go paint the sign." She headed out of the kitchen and into the pantry off the hall. She shut the heavy door, pulled the chain to the naked light bulb in the ceiling, and watched the bulb swing back and forth with the motion. Dim light strobed cans and boxes of foods, jars of spices, and folded table linens on the shelves—and cobwebs in the corners. On a bottom shelf was an unpainted wooden cutout of a figure holding a platter. Radello had special-ordered it from Sunnydale High School's woodshop class, much to Allison's chagrin. One of Allison's many duties was to paint it to look like Zeus with a tray of squid, then hang it over the front door of the restaurant so passers-by would know this was a dining establishment that served genuine Greek cuisine.

"The man is unbelievable!" she hissed to the featureless wooden god. "He has *one* dream that he is meant to be a chef, and he believes it! Buys this old house and converts it into a restaurant. Probably used my college funds to do it. And where does that leave me? Stuck in the middle, as always. He has the dream. I get the nightmare."

She walked over to the window and snapped the shade up. Outside, the sun was shining. Although the window overlooked an alley, when Allison pressed her cheek to the glass, she could see the road to the left. It was late Wednesday afternoon, and the citizens of Sunnydale were doing late-Wednesday-afternoon Sunnydale stuff. Cars whizzed back and forth. A couple across the road gazed into the window of Erin's Irish Antiques. Students from Sunnydale High strolled by on their way to the mall. There were Ben Rothman and Sanford Jennings, both burly and not-bad-looking seniors on the high-school wrestling team. Then came a group of popular girls led by the perfectly dressed Cordelia Chase who, of course, never gave the gangly, awkward Allison Gianakous the time of day because Cordelia was way in and Allison was pretty much totally out. A few loners came afterward, and then Allison saw Buffy Summers, Xander Harris, and Willow Rosenberg. They were chatting casually, oblivious of the fact that one of their classmates was now destined to spend every free hour in a smelly, smoky restaurant with her *so*-can't-cook father.

"It's not fair!" Allison said, her words making the glass steam. She dropped down on a metal stepstool and clenched her fists. Her father had always run her life. Allison's mother had died when Allison was three, and Radello Gianakous had run the family the way he thought was right—which meant that Allison's brother and father pretty much got to do what they wanted and

Allison didn't. Radello had owned a hardware store, a golf shop, done insurance sales, and now this. Allison's brother Alex got to play sports, go to movies, and stay out all night if he wanted, even while he was in high school.

But not Allison. She had to come home right after school. The only time she got to go to the mall was with her father. No clubs, no movies, no parties. No wonder she had no friends. Radello still ached from the loss of his wife, and Allison knew he thought he was being protective in a weird way, but it wasn't right to make her suffer for it. When was her turn going to come to try new things? Sometimes she felt like a sledgehammer was whacking her on the head, slamming her deeper and deeper into the ground. Soon, she wouldn't be there anymore.

"There has got to be a way out of this," she moaned. "I need help!"

Through the wall, Allison could hear her father singing some off-tune ballad. Sure, *he* was happy.

Allison got up from the stool and ran her hand over the smooth wood of the Zeus-'n'-Squid cutout, then spied the paperback Greek–English, English–Greek dictionary standing beside it. Allison had bought it for her father in case a customer came in who actually spoke Greek. But he'd stuck it back here in storage. Only then did Allison realize that Radello—though he might be able to speak a few Greek words—couldn't read it any more than he could fly to the moon.

Or cook.

She opened the dictionary to "help, call for." The Greek was "ζητῶ βοήθεια." She took an order pad and pen and scribbled the term on the top sheet. She looked up "goddess," but found only "god."

"Figures," she said. "One of those stupid abridged dictionaries."

Then she found the words for feminine and spirit and copied them beside the call for help.

"ζητῶ βοήθεια πνεῦμα θηλμχός."

She said in a whisper, "Help me, goddess."

It sounded ridiculous. The gods and goddesses were those goofy characters she'd painted on the walls of the dining room. There were no such things as real gods and goddesses.

Were there?

Allison shook out a white linen tablecloth, and draped herself toga-style. She made a circle on the floor with cans of olives, shakers of garlic powder, and some dried fig leaves. She stood in the circle then, holding the slip of order paper up toward the ceiling. "Help me, goddess," she said. "Any goddess will do, I don't care." She giggled, then stopped.

She was of Greek heritage. These were the deities of her culture. *Why shouldn't I take them seriously?* It was worth a try. Besides, if it didn't work no one would know she'd made an idiot out of herself.

She lowered her head and closed her eyes. She slowed her breathing, concentrating every muscle and nerve in her body to the request she was making.

"Help me, goddess."

Help me help me help me help me.

She waited, she listened. In the kitchen, her father was slamming pans around.

Help me help me help me.

And then there was something. A brief caress of cool, rose-scented air, and the paper in her hand trembled. But that was all. No spectral form bearing a laurel wreath and good tidings.

She waited, listening.

But there was nothing else—if there had really been a breeze in the first place. "Goddess?" she whispered, suddenly feeling stupid again.

But the only voice was her father's, calling for help with a tray of pastries he had just dropped.

She untangled herself from the tablecloth, replaced the cans, and hurried to the kitchen.

CHAPTER 1

The night smelled of death; of rotting leaves, muck, and small things that had crawled to the side of the country road, twisted pitifully, and given up the ghost. It had rained earlier, and filmy puddles stood in the ruts of the road's surface, reflecting a sharp, sliver moon. The silent wind was cold.

Brian Andrews stood alone by the road in the darkness, hands drawn up in the sleeves of his basketball-letter jacket, furious with his friends for dumping him out of the car ten minutes earlier, when he'd said the inside of the car stank like gym clothes and dog crap. They'd hauled the car up short, popped the door, and pushed Brian out, saying, "Good luck sniffing out a better ride, chief!", then peeled rubber on the gravel, the red tail lights and their howling laughter fading in the distance.

Brian had grabbed a handful of gravel and hurled it at the receding car, but it fell short, and seconds later he was alone in the dark. With the sickle moon watching.

"You pathetic, brain-dead jocks!" he yelled down the empty road. "Just try to come back for me and you'll

wish you hadn't! I'll show you what I think of your attitude!"

The only answer came from the crickets in the road-
side weeds and the distorted banjo voices of bullfrogs in
a nearby pond.

"You guys are sucky ballplayers, anyway, anybody
ever tell you that? You play like girls! Ha!"

Nothing.

Brian tugged up his collar and looked around, not be-
lieving he had no way back to Sunnydale. He had never
walked in his life, at least not to really *get* anywhere. He
always had a car or a ride. Only losers were reduced to
using footpower to go places. His own car was in the
shop for a cracked engine mount, but his friends—well,
those idiots up the road who *used* to be his friends—always had a couple of working vehicles between them.

"Now what?" he demanded out loud. He didn't care,
fine, he'd sit on the side of the road and die before he'd
walk back to Sunnydale. Let Charlie and Greg have it on
their heads that he was dead. He was totally and completely not going to walk back. It had to be a whole mile
or two away at least.

It was as if his demand was worthy of a divine answer,
for at that moment, a white Volkswagen beetle came
over the ridge, glowing in the moonlight, and slid to a
stop. The driver's side window rolled down, revealing an
incredible blond babe with huge blue eyes and a smile
that went on forever. A pleasant whiff of perfume drifted
across the space between them.

"Good evening," said the girl. "Am I to presume you
have lost your way?"

"Huh?"

She laughed lightly and waved him over. Her nails
were painted pink, as were her lips. On her wrist was a

sparkling bracelet, set with what appeared to be real diamonds. She was the ultimate—no ifs, ands, or buts—and Brian was already imagining himself twenty minutes from now, her mouth on his, his hands on her. "I believe you could use some help. Please, be my guest."

Like I'm gonna turn this down! Brian thought hungrily.

He trotted around the front of the car, climbed into the passenger's seat, and immediately threw his arm across the back of the seat and put his feet—which were attached to very long legs—up on the dashboard for more space, so she would know he was the casual type. If the babe minded she didn't say so. She tossed her long golden hair back from her shoulders and asked, "So where do you want to go?"

Brian shrugged. "Wherever," he said. "Wherever you want to go. *Babe.*" He winked, letting her know he was a man with confidence. *Man, she smells great!*

The girl laughed lightly, and touched his cheek.

Ah, yeah, he thought. *This is going to be really fine. It must have been the good will of the gods for Charlie and Greg to kick me out of their car!*

The girl jammed the stick shift into gear and drove for a half-mile without speaking. Brian paced himself according to his past successes. If he acted too early, she might pitch him from the car like his ex-friends had. And so he made small talk.

"Got twenty-eight points in our last game."

No response.

"Nice car. No offense or anything but mine's better. Got a Lexus."

Nada.

"I work out. I pump, lift. I'm pretty buff under these clothes."

The girl only smiled.

"What's your name?" he asked.

"What's in a name?" she answered without looking over.

"Um, I don't know." He fiddled with the radio. "Where's your CD player?"

"Ah, but you see, I make my own music."

She then pulled off the road onto a rutted dirt pathway and drove to the side of a small lake, the car bouncing all the way. Then she cut the engine and the lights. She stared ahead through the windshield, her pink-nailed fingers strumming silently, the bracelet sparkling with a distant, unknown light. Outside, cattails and marsh reeds stood like sentinels along the lake's edge, shivering in a breeze. Little creature-eyes blinked from between the stalks.

The parked car was Brian's cue. But she beat him to it, turning to him before he turned to her, taking his face in her hands, and running a pointed nail along the bridge of his nose. "You are a most impressive young man," she said softly, her breath cool and sweet like the inside of a flower shop.

"Yeah? I mean yeah."

Totally and supremely fine this is!

She traced her fingers down his face, then into his hair. As she leaned into him and kissed his neck, he thought, *Just wait 'til I tell Charlie and Greg about this, those guys will wish they'd kicked themselves out of that stinking car. Those idiots, they're gonna . . .*

But then she began to hum in his ear, a soft, soothing melody he'd never heard before, and his thoughts drained from his mind like pudding down a disposal. He pulled back from her, shaking his head to clear it, wondering if the overload of salsa-drenched hot dogs he'd had for supper was catching up with him. But he didn't feel sick, just calm.

A little dizzy, but very, very calm.

This is great, he thought, leaning back toward her. *I'm a stud, I'm a hot exhaust pipe, she could see that from the side of the . . .*

She put her mouth back to his ear and began to hum again, and the thoughts ran out, warm and easy. In their place came a trembling sensation in the pit of his stomach that felt a lot like seasickness. Fingernails dug long scratches down his neck that burned like fire. He tried to pull away but couldn't remember how to. He tried to speak but couldn't think of what to say.

There was something wet on his shoulders. It was coming out of his ears, thick and runny. *What . . . ?* he thought, but that thought slid away, too. The tune grew louder in his head, disorienting and totally weird. He felt he might be in some kind of trouble, but couldn't be sure.

And then he was being dragged from the car, his head bumping across rocks and through razor grass, and was dropped into the lake.

He was sinking into the slime and the goose grease and the algae, and could no longer breathe. . . . He was drowning. The rancid water was flooding his mouth and making him gag, making him kick and thrash, but he could not for the life of him remember how to swim.

And as his insides began to burn with a lack of air, as his lungs screamed and imploded, and as his teeth, on their own accord, began to gnaw his tongue to shreds in feeble, agonized helplessness, he heard her. From up past the scummy surface of lake her musical voice was calling after him, "Give my regards to Charon!"

* * *

The Laughing Greek was the newest restaurant in town, and at first glance seventeen-year-old Buffy Summers was pretty sure it would also be the next one to go belly-up. Tonight was opening night, with offers of "buy-one, get-one-free" entrees, but from the looks of things through the plate-glass window on the street side, it seemed as if Sunnydale had decided to pretend it didn't exist. Sad, but not a surprise. The smells from inside were enough to curl nose hairs. And not in a good way.

Buffy's friend Xander Harris had had a two-month-long crush on a beautiful Greek exchange student last year, during which time he had developed what he insisted was a well-honed affinity for Greek food; thus he had insisted they all go to show their civic support of the new establishment.

"I can just sit back, smell the simmering olive oil, and remember Helena," Xander said as he, Buffy, and their friends Willow and Oz met on the sidewalk in front of the restaurant's front door. "Nice sign."

Above the door dangled a painted wooden man in an orange tunic-thing holding a pan of lumpy, sizzling *something*. His head was topped with a puke-green laurel wreath, and he was smiling so broadly Buffy was reminded of the Cheshire cat. *A very demented, lopsided Cheshire cat.*

"I wonder who the artist was?" asked pretty, auburn-haired Willow Rosenberg with her usual hopeful smile. She was wearing orange sneakers, jeans, and a very fuzzy pink sweater. "It's kind of free and expressive, isn't it? Kind of cute like that Pizza-Pizza guy, only scary?"

"Hey," said Oz, Willow's musician boyfriend. He was dressed as formally as he ever got—a Gumby tee beneath an unbuttoned shirt. "What's up?" He hooked one thumb in the back pocket of his baggy cargo pants and draped the other arm over Willow's shoulder.

"My mom's cooking at home tonight," said Xander. *"My* mom? Cooking? *Hello?* This place has to serve something better than one of Mama Harris's 'I am woman, see me poach' creations."

Buffy ran a strand of blond hair behind her ear, then shoved her hands into the pockets of her leather jacket. Inside, she could feel the smooth, thick pieces of wood she had brought with her just in case. Sometimes, with the day-to-day dilemmas she and her friends faced, she could almost, sometimes, forget for the briefest fraction of a second that she was the Vampire Slayer, and that it was she and she alone who stood between the demons of the night and the rest of humanity.

"Xander," she said, "breathe. Inhale, or whatever it is a Harris does to absorb oxygen. Can you smell that? It stinks! Do you honestly think it's safe in there?"

"This is Sunnydale," Xander scoffed. "You tell me."

"Xander . . . ," complained Buffy.

"Just humor me. It's for old time's sake. It's a little nostalgia for the Xan-man, to bring back a memory of long legs in the desk next to mine in chemistry class, tucked as far away from me as she could possibly get them, her face showing every ounce of disgust she felt for me—but next to mine anyway. The beautiful Helena, as mesmerizing as the goddess Diana."

"Diana was Roman, not Greek," said Willow.

"Whatever. Come on," said Xander. He tugged open the door. "The smells are probably distorted through a Sunnydale dimension warp or something. Let's eat!"

There was a single dining room inside, with the walls painted to resemble ancient Athens. On one wall, the

Parthenon was slathered in accents of purple and lime. On the opposite wall were a bunch of peach-colored naked Olympians—running, jumping, and wrestling, all with legs conveniently placed to pass this as a family dining establishment. The third wall, which contained the front window, was decorated with lime and blue grapevines, and the back wall, where the kitchen door opened, was painted with a slew of indistinguishable goddesses and gods peeking out from a cloudy Mt. Olympus. Some crockery—most likely from Bargain Bazaar at the mall—was on a shelf over the front door.

Buffy, Oz, Xander, and Willow stood in the middle of the room, the only patrons in the place. There was no host. No waiter, either.

"Hello!" called Xander. "Buy-one-get-one-free! We have arrived!"

Oz ran one hand through his hair. "Xander, I'm thinking pizza. I have band practice in two hours."

"Listen," said Xander. "We decided it was fair to take turns deciding what to do on a Friday night. It's my turn."

"It's a way poor turn," said Buffy, taking off her jacket. "A wrong turn, a U-turn, a—"

"Shh," said Willow, her voice low. "Someone's coming."

"Hi!" Through the kitchen door came a girl wearing a white apron over a flouncy floral skirt and a laurel wreath drawn up around her brown ponytail. It was Allison Gianakous, fellow student at Sunnydale High. She was a gangly, awkward girl who had no friends Buffy knew of. "I mean good evening!"

"Allison, hi," said Buffy, making herself grin. It felt like such a lie. "So. Newest Greek restaurant in Sunnydale. How about that."

"*Only* Greek restaurant in Sunnydale, in case you didn't know," said Allison, showing the four to a table by the naked Olympians. "My dad thought it was time the Greeks made a statement, culinarily speaking that is."

"Sure, yeah, time it is," said Willow. She folded her hands on the tabletop and nodded enthusiastically. "Smells great!"

Buffy gave Willow an *I can't believe you said that* look, but Willow refused to look back.

"We've only been open an hour," said Allison, shrugging and tipping her head in the direction of the empty tables. "I bet we'll fill up soon. You think so?"

"Sure," said Xander.

"Sure," said Willow.

Oz scratched his head.

"Oh god—we won't!" said Allison, her smile collapsing into a scowl of dismay. She dropped into a chair at the next table. "This was such a major mistake! Who are we kidding? My father can't cook!"

"Can anybody's parents cook?" asked Xander.

Allison grabbed the laurel wreath in her fingers and yanked it down around her neck. It looked for a moment like she was going to hang herself, right there in front of everyone, with a bunch of leaves wrapped around coathanger wire. "This sucks!"

"I'm sure it's not as bad as you think," offered Buffy. "Really. Want me to hold that wreath for you before you—well, want me to hold it?"

"But it *is* that bad," said Allison. She let go of the wreath and clenched one fist inside the other. "My father would kill me if he heard me say this, but anyone who takes a whiff will know the truth. Do you all have really bad colds or something?"

"I like the tablecloths," said Xander. "They're all white and pressed and stuff. Like in a real restaurant."

A booming male voice came from the other room. "Allison! We have guests? Turn on the music! Make sure they know the specials! And don't forget the water!"

"Yes, Dad," Allison called back, jumping to her feet and pulling a handful of menus from her big apron pocket. She looked Buffy in the eye. "My family's lived in Sunnydale since I was born, and the only Greek food we ate were gyros. Then my father gets a bug up his you-know-what and decides he should be a chef and I should learn my culture."

Xander shivered visibly. "Culture!"

"Allison?" Mr. Gianakous's face appeared at the door. "You tell 'em the specials?"

"Yes, sir, Dad!"

"And water first. Where is the water?"

"I'm getting it!" Allison's jaw clenched visibly as her father pulled back into the kitchen. "The restaurant's bad enough. But the main thing is . . . my father."

"You don't have to tell us this if it makes you uncomfortable," said Buffy, hoping it would make Allison uncomfortable because she felt it was going to get really personal really quickly.

But Allison continued. "Men!" she said, her voice lowered. "Always wanting their own way, doing their little power thing, flexing their testosterone. My grandfather. My brother. My father. I'm so sick of it!"

"Well, I don't know," began Willow. "It's not like it used to be. We're all equal, who doesn't know that, and I know some females who can whup some pretty good . . . who are like, well, pretty powerful and all."

Allison wasn't listening. "Just don't get me started! *Don't* get me started! Dad doesn't even consider me human. I'm a *girl,* after all! He's got this old-school attitude, and I can't handle it anymore! He expects to do what he wants, that I don't want anything at all. Selfish much? Taking my life away much? I'm not going to be taken advantage of—I'm going to prove myself as a real woman soon, a powerful woman, just wait and see!"

In unison, Buffy, Willow, Oz, and Xander said, "Okay."

"Now," said Allison, trying to brighten. "Specials are the saganaki—fried cheese; the plaki—baked fish with garlic; and the pastitsio—kind of a lasagna thing. These are specials 'cause you get free melitzanosalata with them. Eggplant dip. With Ritz Bits. Dad couldn't quite get the Greek bread to rise."

They left The Laughing Greek two hours after arriving, all with doggy bags containing the majority of the uneaten meals. Night had fallen with a vengeance, and the streetlights on the road struggled just to give off the barest puddles of illumination in the gloom.

Oz immediately crammed his bag into the nearest street-side trashcan.

"Amazing," Xander said. "Mr. Gianakous and my mother could have a bakeoff and they'd both lose."

Willow looked at her bag, then threw it in with Oz's. She said woefully, "All that effort for such small results."

"And Mr. Gianakous has plans for expansion!" said Xander with horrified wonder. "Did you hear that? He wants to make the empty banquet room into a dance floor so his place can compete with The Bronze. Quite the dazed dreamer."

"Poor Allison." Buffy sighed deeply, and with a flick of her wrist flipped her doggy bag full of plaki through the air and into the garbage. *No rim.* She drew her jacket in around her. The air had chilled with the setting of the sun. "She looks like she's ready to crawl out of her skin. Her father did nothing but boss her around all night like she was an idiot. It would drive me crazy!"

"Xander," Oz said. "Hope you realize what we did for you tonight."

"And you won't let me live it down, will you?" he asked. "You'll add this to your make-fun-of-Xander repertoire, along with the got-old-real-fast she-mantis jokes."

Willow and Oz bid Buffy and Xander good-bye, then climbed into Oz's van, which was parked two spaces down. Oz was a guitar player for the ultra-on band Dingoes Ate My Baby, and it was a passion to him as strong as any calling. He might not be much into academics, as bright as he was, but he was never late for anything that had to do with music. And he was good.

Well, Buffy thought as Oz's van coughed into consciousness, *at least he has a choice in life—his calling. At least he doesn't have to put his life in danger every day to save those around him, unless people begin dropping dead for lack of a good strong G chord.*

"Hey," said Xander.

Yeah, well, Buffy thought as the van pulled from the curb and disappeared into the darkness, *Oz does turn into a werewolf a few days a month, but what female doesn't know the grouchy side of a cycle? I wouldn't mind trading stakes for drooling fangs once in a while!*

"Hey, Buffy, wanna go to The Bronze?"

Buffy shook her head. "I've had enough for tonight."

"Don't want to dance with me? You *know* I can move!"

"Oh, I don't doubt that for a second. But—no thanks. Besides, I have to make with the patrol."

Xander made a clucking sound, then turned and walked off, still clutching his crumpled doggy bag to his chest, as if by sheer will he could make the contents transcend from something hellish into something heavenly.

Buffy gave one last glance at The Laughing Greek, and saw Allison at the window. Her face looked warped behind the uneven glass, but Buffy knew she couldn't be smiling. Surely she'd seen the doggy bags take a nose dive. Surely she'd seen the grimaces of her fellow Sunnydale High-ers.

With a tentative smile and a wave, Buffy hurried down the walk to the edge of the block. She turned north, moving into the alley. It was a shorter walk home this way, although she knew she was inviting the possibility of a demon encounter. Vampires loved the community of Sunnydale, as did a steady stream of other evil beings. This Southern California town was a vortex for supernatural badness.

And the night shadows of Sunnydale's myriad alleyways were a favorite hangout for the demons du jour.

Well, I haven't exactly done my required vampire patrol tonight, she thought. *I need something to report tomorrow. Might as well start here.*

As Buffy reached the middle of the alley, she saw two dark figures approaching. Silently and deftly, she dropped behind a stack of cardboard boxes and pulled the two wooden stakes from the pocket of her jacket. She was not afraid; two vampires and two stakes, it didn't get any better than that. Just two quick jabs through their hearts and she could be home in time for *Dark Shadows* reruns.

Her nerves were steeled, her muscles coiled and ready. Her Watcher had trained her well.

She leaped from behind the boxes, stakes raised, a war-whoop howling from her throat. And then she stopped dead in her tracks. "Oh—oops," she said sheepishly. "Hi there."

Rupert Giles, the librarian at Sunnydale High, skidded to a halt in the gravel, springing into a karate stance, his hands up in front of his chest. His female companion gasped. Both their eyes were huge and white in the shadows.

"Buffy!" exclaimed Giles in his dignified English accent, his hands still holding their you-move-you-lose position, his glasses knocked askew on his nose. "And to what do we attribute such a fine welcome this evening?"

Now isn't this just the best case scenario, Buffy thought grimly. Not only was Giles the librarian, he was also her Watcher, the wise soul who was responsible for her Slayer training and education. No one knew his true identity—or Buffy's—except Buffy herself and a small circle that included Xander, Willow, Oz, and—unfortunately for the most part—the self-centered, snobby high-school beauty named Cordelia Chase.

This surprise attack had to have looked pretty darn shoddy.

Buffy quickly drew the stakes in close to her side, dropping them into her pocket. She wondered if the woman with Giles—a tall, very attractive, slender lady with well-coiffed black hair—had actually seen the weapons.

"Well, Giles," said Buffy as the Watcher lowered his hands and adjusted his glasses. "You are the last person I expected to find here—now, tonight on this side of town, walking in an alley."

"Well, here I am," he said, giving Buffy one of his piercing, corrective gazes. "And there you are, doing some kind of alley dance?" He was covering for her. He knew she was patrolling, but there was no way he'd let the black-haired beauty know the truth.

"I—" said Buffy. "I thought you were Xander. You don't know Xander," she said to the woman, "but if you did you'd know he needs a little shock every once in a while to keep him alert. Yes, not often alert, that's our Xander. I was doing the keep-Xander-alert thing. He's not exactly narcoleptic, but close. Worse, actually—"

"Mr. Giles," said the woman. Her voice was all pinched and hoity-toity. It made Buffy cringe. "Who might this delightful, energetic young lady be?"

"Ms. Moon, this is Buffy Summers, a senior at the high school, and one of our brightest, most talented students. Buffy, this is Ms. Mo Moon, the new supervisor for school libraries in Sunnydale. She paid a surprise visit after school today—and what a *surprise* it was— and suggested we take a serious look at the contents of our library. She thinks we might want to reconsider our *offerings,* such as the books on the supernatural and the unexplained. How about that?" Buffy could see the distaste on Giles's stoic face, just below the surface. But she knew no one else could have detected it. Giles was amazing that way. "I invited her to the new Greek restaurant," he continued, "where I thought we could discuss things more freely in a relaxed atmosphere. Good food, good drink."

"You're going to The Laughing Greek?" Buffy asked.

"Why yes," said Giles. "Why do you ask it that way?"

"Oh," said Buffy with a shrug, thinking she should warn him, but then—the woman had such a haughty air of superiority, maybe a trip to The Laughing Greek would be just the thing to pop that air bubble just a little. "I'd like to hear your take on it Monday. It's new, you know. Newest restaurant in town. 'Buy-one, get-one-free.'"

"I've heard," said Giles. From his expression, she knew she'd have some major explaining to do on Monday. Why she hadn't been able to tell, with her well-trained Slayer senses, that Giles was human, not monster. Why she didn't warn Giles and the black-haired woman about the killer fare at The Laughing Greek.

"Nice to meet you, Mrs. Moon."

"That is *Ms.* Moon, my dear."

Whatever. "Yes, well," said Buffy. "Have fun." Buffy hurried up the alley, the stakes clacking in her pocket.

I can't believe I wasn't paying enough attention to sense Giles was a friend and not a foe, Buffy thought as she reached the end of the alley, and stopped to readjust the stakes. A tattered gray cat looked at her from on top of an abandoned pile of truck tires. *I'm tired of having to always be so diligent. I want to be careless and unaware, like other people my age.*

And then she did smell it, or feel it—to the very core of her being. The prickling along her spine, the static sensation that brought the hairs on her arms to attention and made her heart beat faster.

They are here.

She glanced up and down the street. A few cars were left on the side of the road, one of them Giles's. He'd probably parked there and made the woman walk with him through the alley just for spite. The woman might be pretty, but Giles could be creatively subtle when he wanted to gain the upper hand.

Buffy tasted the air with her sixth sense. They were close, very close.

Vampires.

She yanked the stakes from her pocket and held the

two between her fingers like massive chopsticks. *Come on, let's get it over with. I don't have all night.*

The car closest to Buffy was a dented blue sedan of questionable parentage. The front and back doors squealed open simultaneously, and four females emerged. Their faces were the furrowed, disfigured countenances of the undead; their eyes glowed, their teeth were sharp and prominent within blood-colored lips. It seemed two of them might have been attractive brunettes in an earlier life. The third had been albino, the fourth a freckled redhead.

Four. Not a good number with just two stakes. Buffy would have to be more inventive to manage this many. Why didn't these guys ever take a night off? Stay home and bake a nice blood pudding or something?

"Slayer," the redhead hissed.

"You got it right," said Buffy, and with one, quick motion, she hurled the first stake through the air. It impaled one of the brunettes through the chest, and she fell to the ground with a grunt and an uncommon look of surprise on her face. She disintegrated immediately into a vampire-shaped pile of dust.

"Get her!" wailed the redhead, clenching her talon-fists and running toward Buffy.

Buffy leaped clear, rolling the second stake in her fingers—a threatening motion to the vampires, a comforting motion for herself. "Get her? Isn't that supposed to be 'kill her'?"

"Shut up, Slayer!" said the redhead as she regained herself and turned to face Buffy again.

The albino glanced over at the pile of dust that had been her companion, which was already spreading in the wind, caught up in a whirlwind and blowing across the road and onto the vehicles lining the curb. She screamed,

"Seize her before she does any more damage!" The three vampires drew together and rushed at Buffy, shoulder-to-shoulder, their teeth snapping, their claws slashing.

Buffy tossed the stake into the air and caught it in her teeth, while in the very same second she spun around on her toes and snatched up two of the tires on which the cat was sitting, sending the feline flying in a hissing ball of fury. She whirled back around and waved the tires.

The vampires froze, looking at Buffy's new weapons.

"Rubber won't cut it, sister!" said the redhead.

These girls don't know how this works, Buffy thought, holding the heavy tires out to either side like enormous cymbals ready to clang. Her muscles complained, but she was strong. Giles insisted she train daily, and so far—with his help and that of Angel, her vampire-with-a-soul boyfriend—her ever-increasing skill in tae kwon do and other Eastern martial art forms had proven as beneficial to her survival as a piece of wood. *This is supposed to be kill or be killed. These demon chicks must be real new to this game if they think the object is to take a hostage!*

The redhead snarled. Her breath was foul, even worse than the inside of The Laughing Greek, and rippled on the night air like a toxin, covering the distance from vampire to human. Buffy tried not to gag. The vampires leaped forward in unison with a shriek.

Buffy sprang up with all her strength, raising the tires over her head and bringing them down so quickly that the albino and the brunette barely had time to blink their undead eyes. But the redhead caught Buffy in the ribs with a well-aimed blow, sending her sprawling to the sidewalk. One of Buffy's tires hit its mark—down over the head and shoulders of the brunette, pinning her arms to her body. The other struck the albino on the head, bounced off, and rolled down the street.

Buffy was up in a second, stake still clamped in her teeth. But she was short of breath and coughing. She jumped up and drove the side of her foot against the face of the redhead, knocking her away with a snarl and then *humph!* grabbed the stake from her teeth and slammed it down into the chest of the tire-bound vampire. The vampire's ugly demon features dissolved into dust and spilled to the ground, the tire holding in the air for a second before falling after her.

Buffy yanked the stake back and sprang aside as the redhead and albino rushed her.

Two and one stake. Not great, but doable.

Now the vampires caught her by the upper arms and slammed her to the walk on her back. Buffy twisted wildly and bucked, throwing the redhead off and aiming the stake toward the heart of the other. But the albino pulled away in time, hopping to her feet beside the redhead, who had regained herself. Buffy sprang upward and jumped back, waving the stake at them both.

"Come on, come on!" Buffy chanted. "Dead-again time!"

But neither came forward. They just stared at her with their inhuman eyes, mouths drooling, teeth gnashing.

"You wait," said the redhead at last. "You just wait . . ."

"Oh, shut up, Viva," growled the albino.

". . . until we catch you, you little snit. You'll be dancing to our tune, you'll see!"

Buffy lunged forward, but the two vampires turned and ran up the street amid the filthy, scattering remains of their former buds.

"What is your problem besides being dead and ugly?"

Buffy called after them, but there was no answer. She turned to the tattered gray cat and said, "Did they say catch? That was supposed to be kill. It doesn't make sense. Does it make sense to you?"

The cat didn't answer, either. It just licked its butt and walked away.

CHAPTER 2

A body had been found in the shallow water at the edge of a small lake on some farmland north of town. The deceased was student Brian Andrews, a basketball player who, at the time of his demise, was not dating anyone important, according to the popular crowd. The police report stated that Brian, likely intoxicated, had wandered into the water, slipped, and drowned.

"Did either of you know Brian very well?" Willow asked Xander and Buffy as the three of them sat at one of the round tables in the bright Sunnydale High cafeteria. Willow was ignoring her lunch while Buffy and Xander picked through pieces of a single decent lunch they had compiled from two mediocre ones—a burrito, an apple half, a pile of barbecue chips, and some stray red grapes. All around them, at other tables and by the walls, students were discussing the latest news. The upcoming Miss Sunnydale High Pageant. The two new girls who had enrolled yesterday. The death of Brian Andrews. Pretty much in that order.

"He was on the basketball team, that's all I know," said Xander. "He wasn't very good."

"That's mean," said Willow. "He's dead, you know."

"I don't mean he died because he wasn't good, but being dead doesn't make him a better player."

"I guess not," Willow mused. She fingered the bracelet her parents had given her for Hanukkah, a gold band with an aquamarine stone; at the moment it sported a new addition, a yellow plastic Three Stooges charm that Oz had gotten her at the arcade. She took a grape from Xander's outstretched hand. "If only he'd been on the swim team, maybe he wouldn't have drowned."

"Willow," said Xander. "The water was only two and a half feet deep."

"That's worse. How embarrassing to drown in two and a half feet when there's a good six feet right next to you?"

Buffy pushed the tray away from her, leaving Xander to scoot it back to himself for the remaining chips. "I met Brian Andrews when I first came to Sunnydale," she said. "Believe it or not, he was nice back then. I was knocked into a wall and dropped my books. He helped me pick them up. I never forgot that."

There was a moment of silence. Then Buffy said, in a low voice only her friends could hear—at Sunnydale High there were big ears everywhere—"I guess one bright note is that this death doesn't seem to have any peculiarities. He was probably drunk and careless. The police didn't report any dual puncture wounds."

"Just some scratches on his neck is what I heard," said Xander. "Fish probably gnawed him."

Buffy nodded. She felt terrible for Brian's family. But at least it wasn't something she as the Slayer could have known about or prevented. Some bad things were actually natural and normal bad things. Maybe this was one of those.

Maybe. In her mind's eye, she saw a smaller and skinnier Brian Andrews grinning at her awkwardly as he helped her clutch her geography and algebra books amid the onslaught of student feet.

"Hi, there!"

Buffy looked around to see Allison Gianakous behind her, a broad smile on her lips.

"Hi, Allison," Buffy said. "How are you doing? Miss the laurel wreath."

"Yeah, well," said Allison. She dropped onto the seat next to Xander, put her elbows on the table, and poked at a remaining apple slice on the communal tray. It was clear she had something on her mind other than a Monday afternoon hello. Allison was not one of Buffy's friends, but she was using all sorts of good-friend body language.

She wanted something.

"What do you want?" This was Xander. He didn't possess the proper finesse for acquiring information delicately.

"Actually," said Allison, "I was hoping you guys would back me up on something."

"What's that?" asked Willow.

"How would you describe me?" asked Allison.

"What do you mean, describe?" asked Buffy.

"If you were going to tell somebody what I looked like, what would you say?"

"Why, you gonna commit a crime?" asked Xander. "You want to go ahead and get the suspect sketch started to save a little time?"

"Come on," said Allison with a roll of her eyes.

"Okay," said Willow. "You have brown hair, brown eyes, no freckles. Uh. . . ."

"Would you say I was pretty?"

Buffy opened her mouth, then snapped it shut. A conversation like this could quickly become about as dangerous as a walk alone in Sunnydale at night. And she didn't want to hurt Allison's feelings. "Ah, well, beauty is in the eye of the beholder," she offered.

"Great *Twilight Zone* episode!" said Xander.

"No, really," said Allison. "Would you say I'm pretty?"

Willow, Xander, and Buffy stared at Allison. Willow said, "Well, sure, Allison. . . ."

"But I'm not," Allison said matter-of-factly. "You wouldn't describe me as pretty, you'd describe me as . . ."

"Tall?" offered Buffy.

"Exactly!" said Allison. "Tall. And how would you describe most successful basketball players?"

"Tall!" said Xander, as enthusiastically as if he'd just answered Final Jeopardy correctly.

"Sure," said Allison, nodding. "You see?"

"Not really," said Buffy.

"But you do," Allison insisted. "I want to show my Dad that I'm not his slave. I want to prove to him I'm as good as my brother. That I have a life and I should live it!"

"Live it how?" asked Buffy.

"I'm going to try out for Brian Andrews's spot on the basketball team!"

Buffy, Willow, and Xander responded in unison: "Not really."

"Why not?" Allison clutched Buffy's arm.

"Oh, I don't know," said Buffy, pulling away as gently

as she could. "Maybe because you're a girl and it's a boys' team?"

Allison shook her head. "Don't you see? That's the point. Who made up these girl-team, boy-team rules? Men did, that's who. I want to challenge that! It's time we of the feminine persuasion of Sunnydale High made our stand and refused to let these rules govern us anymore!"

"I've never felt governed by a male-female rule thing," said Willow carefully. "At least I don't think I have."

"You're behind by a few years, Allison," said Xander. "It's women who rule the world now, just look at Xena. Mary Kate and Ashley. Do you *know* what those kids make? And then there's—" But he stopped short as Buffy gave him a watch-what-you're-saying glare.

Allison was not listening. "I heard the two new girls say something about coed teams, how our school should have them. It got me to thinking, why not me? So I asked Principal Snyder before school if I could try out."

"And he said . . . ?" said Willow.

"No, of course," said Allison.

"That's too bad," said Buffy. She hopped up, dragging her backpack from the table and slinging it over her shoulder. Xander and Willow followed suit. "But it was a nice idea. See you guys later. Class in five."

"Wait, Buffy," said Allison. "If you all come with me when I ask again, he might say yes. Power in numbers. And if he doesn't, he'll know that we've got a cause here!"

Buffy threw up one hand and headed for the cafeteria door. Other students were migrating in the same direction. "Allison," she said over her shoulder. "I'm really sorry, but I'm pretty much all caused-out at the moment.

Maybe you can find somebody else who is into that coed-teams thing."

"Who?"

"Oh, I don't know. The two new girls, maybe? New kids always get more administrative consideration." She paused. "At least for a while."

"But I don't know them," said Allison.

Buffy gave Willow a frustrated glance. Willow raised one brow and blew out a silent breath, her expression speaking clearly—*We treated Allison like a friend the other night at The Laughing Greek. So now are we supposed to act like we don't care?* Xander's attention was long gone, latched to the short, bouncing skirt of a sophomore in front of him. Allison trotted after the three of them.

In the hall, students moved around each other in tight quarters, most of them trying not to bump against someone who wasn't of their breeding or station, some of those of lesser breeding or station intentionally bumping into those who were trying their best to ignore them, just for fun. Buffy veered off from her friends, moving down the hall that passed the school's main office, trying to outstride Allison. But the other girl's legs were more than long enough to keep up. Buffy decided not to stop at her locker; it would only give Allison the chance to hang there and complain some more.

And then Buffy was jerked to a stop in front of the door to the office. Allison had grabbed her arm. Buffy yanked away. "Allison!" she said with all the control she could muster. "Cut it out. I can't help you with this. Okay? You might not know it but I would do more harm than good if—"

"Okay," said Allison. "I'll leave you alone. Right after we talk to Principal Snyder. Principal Snyder!"

The principal, a short, balding man, was coming out through the office door holding a scrawny freshman boy by the collar. He paused to look at Allison as the freshman twisted like a fish on a line. "What do you want?" he demanded.

"I'm here with a witness," said Allison, crossing her arms. She was a good three inches taller than Snyder, and at a distance she might have looked convincing, but Buffy could see her arms trembling. "Buffy Summers thinks I should be allowed to try out for the boys' basketball team, and so do I. I'm asking again, Principal Snyder. Will you let me try for Brian Andrews's basketball position?"

Principal Snyder looked from Allison to Buffy and back again, his face changing from a snarl to a bemused yet cold smile. "*Buffy Summers* is your champion? I would chose more wisely, Miss Gianakous," he said. "Miss Summers has had her share of troubles here, if you didn't know. Now, if you'll excuse me, I've got a graffiti artist to put in detention."

Allison was fighting back tears. "But—" she began.

"But no, Miss Gianakous," the principal called over his shoulder as he tugged the freshman along. "You may not try for the boys' basketball team. It's one thing to be equal, it's another to hit a two-pointer outside the zone."

Allison stared after him with a look of fury and dismay. Buffy sighed, touched her shoulder, and said, "Hey, sorry. I tried to tell you I wasn't exactly the principal's golden child. But it's not like the end of the world."

Allison's fists clenched. "Oh no, Buffy? Oh *no*? Just whose world are you talking about?" Then she shoved her way through the mob of students, disappearing only when several members of the boys' basketball team moved in behind her, obscuring the top of her head.

Buffy hadn't met the two new girls yet, but Cordelia made sure she didn't miss the opportunity. It had been a long Monday, and all Buffy wanted to do this afternoon was to go home, recuperate from the pop quiz she had bungled in government class, eat a granola bar, and flip through the new college brochures that had most likely come in the mail before night fell and she'd have to go back on evening patrol. It was amazingly curious how colleges from all over the United States could find one not-all-that-academically-impressive high school senior in Sunnydale, California and decide that they wanted *her,* and *her* in particular, to apply to their fine institution. More often than not, the very personal letters that came with the colorful brochures didn't know her quite as well as they claimed to—they thought she was Buffy Sommers, Buffy Simmers, Becky Sumner, Biffy Summit, Buffet Sondheim—and once, Boffy Sumac.

Buffy stepped out of the school into the Sunnydale sunshine, slipping on her shades and stretching her shoulders. Out in the student parking lot, cars were revving and heading for the street. Buffy could see Oz and Willow standing beside his van, talking and laughing. Xander was leaning against the back of the vehicle, reading a comic book. Usually Buffy would hang out with them after school, but today she just wanted to crash.

"There you are! Why don't you just be invisible all day?"

Buffy looked behind her to see Cordelia Chase scowling with one hand on her hip. Cordelia was a pretty girl—pretty obnoxious, pretty snobby. She was one of the school's elite, if you wanted to make a bell curve based on in-ness and not much else. Her clothes were always immaculate, her hair and makeup without flaw. It was only when she opened her mouth to speak that the image of perfection, like Jericho's walls, came atumblin' down. With Cordelia were several girls of her elite set and two well-dressed girls Buffy didn't know.

"Cordy," said Buffy. "Why would you take the trouble to track me down? It's just not you."

"Oh," said Cordelia. "But it *is* me. I must introduce our new students, Polly and Calli Moon, to every element in our school, so they know what's what. Back in middle school our science class went on a field trip to the La Brea Tar Pits. You wouldn't remember because you were in Los Angeles, at some other school." She flipped her hand dismissively. "Anyway, the guides showed us where to walk and where not to walk, so we wouldn't get sucked down into the pits like those sloths and woolly mammary things."

"So I'm a tar pit and you guys are giant ground sloths?"

"Well, yeah, something like that," said Cordelia. "Polly and Calli need to know where it's safe to walk, and I have to point out everything to them, since they're new."

"Oh," said Buffy. She gave the new girls a quick perusal, not enough for them to think she really cared about any of Cordy's inane explanations. They looked like twins and were gorgeous, with long blond hair, green eyes, and fair skin. They wore cheerful smiles, and actually looked rather harmless if one didn't consider the company they were keeping. Each wore ruby stud earrings and diamond tennis bracelets. Clearly, these girls were from a family with money. The only things that seemed to be outside of Cordelia's sense of style were the girls' too-strong perfume and their relaxed demeanor. It had almost an old-fashioned feel to it. Courteous. Like people used to be back in the old days when there were manners.

Calli and Polly, Cordelia explained briefly, were sisters, a junior and senior respectively—which ruled out the twin assumption, unless one of them had been held back somewhere in a past grade. They drove way cool, way cute Volkswagen beetles—Polly had a white one, Calli a yellow one. And like Cordelia, the Moon girls were considering being contestants in the Miss Sunnydale High Pageant, to be held at the end of the month in the school auditorium. It was being sponsored by Wayland Software Enterprises, a Los Angeles company that was hoping to build an industrial park in Sunnydale.

"This pageant," Cordy continued with a grin that said to Buffy, *Let these two enter, I've got it all over them!,* "is going to be so much better than other pathetic pageants. One thing that's better is that the main purpose isn't to parade beautiful girls around like cattle—although that's okay, too. The main reason is to show off the many talents and abilities of Sunnydale's young women."

"Like you," said Buffy.

"Of course like me," said Cordy. "I'm a prime example. But the best thing about this pageant is that it doesn't offer a lame scholarship as first prize. Wayland Software Enterprises is giving away a trip to Hawaii!"

"Well, Cordy," said Buffy. "We'll miss you terribly when you sail off to the South Seas with your crown, but somehow we'll survive the loss." She turned and walked away. She could hear Cordelia grumbling behind her. Ms. Chase didn't like walkers-away when she was talking.

In the teachers' parking lot, Giles was standing, keys

in hand, staring into space as if someone had knocked the breath out of him. *I hope it's nothing terrible!* Buffy thought as she raced over to him.

"Giles, what is it?" she asked as she slid to a stop beside him. "Vampires? Ghouls? Sea monsters? Ghosts?"

"Library supervisor," said Giles grimly. His eyes came into focus and he looked at Buffy. His jaw was set and his brows were drawn together. "I shouldn't complain about my job to anyone, not even you, but that woman is unreal. She has gone through the volumes in my library and is insisting we get in line with other high schools in the district."

"Which means?"

"Which means, in Mo Moon's oh-so-professional words, 'restocking the library with worthwhile literature on music, poetry, and theater, and getting rid of the supernatural garbage.' "

"Uh-oh. Wait 'til she gets to the hardcore stuff in your personal collection!"

"Indeed. The woman has no idea of what she is speaking, and I will never allow her to make the changes she is after. She has told me she is only acting supervisor, that the job is only hers for the year, and I'll be damned—pardon my French—if any acting *anybody* is going to meddle in affairs of which they have no inkling."

"Yeah," said Buffy. "Whatever. I agree, one hundred percent."

"She's one odd woman," said Giles with a shake of his head. "I will not take direction from her, regardless of what my job description and her job description say."

"Right," said Buffy. "By the way, does she have two daughters who just enrolled here? Calli and Polly Moon?"

Giles nodded. "Pretty girls. Quite bright, I hear. One is an especially talented singer, the other an exceptional poet. I don't know more than that."

"Neither do I," said Buffy. "And I probably won't, since Cordelia's crowd has decided to take them in and we'll rarely cross paths. Intentionally. Hey, is there anything I can do for you about the library mess?"

"No, no. I just have to collect my thoughts and energy. This isn't a job for the Slayer, it's a job for . . ."

"Superwatcher."

Giles sighed. "My thought exactly. Have a good afternoon. And a good evening. Be watchful. Be careful."

"I will," she said.

As Giles climbed into his car, Buffy thought maybe she should have mentioned that it seemed as if several vampires had wanted to catch her last night. When she'd reported to him this morning, she had been able to give only the briefest of debriefings because Mo Moon was hanging so close in the library. And now Giles seemed so bummed about the supervisor's invasion of his space. She let it go.

Besides, she thought, *even though it was way unusual, I handled the grab-happy vamps. I doubt they'll try it again. I came, I slayed, I vanquished.*

Done deal.

"Buffy . . . !" The voice was soft but very desperate.

Buffy spun around at the calling of her name, her heart picking up a fast rhythm, but saw no one coming her way or waving her over, just students meandering, teachers clustered and talking together, birds picking at insects in the grass. *My imagination,* she thought. *Residual Laughing Greek–fume brain distortion. I've gotta get a grip.* But then she was suddenly struck with a flash image of Brian Andrews lying dead in a shallow pond, then one of him helping her with her books several years ago—kneeling on the floor, scooping them up, and trying to make an impression on her.

She shook the image away, but decided to stop by the card shop on the way home and send a sympathy card to his parents.

There was something better at home for a snack than store-bought granola bars. Homemade lemon-poppy muffins. Buffy's mother, Joyce, had actually come home early from work and was banging around in the kitchen when Buffy came through the front door. Wonderful smells of baking wafted through the living room as Buffy stepped inside.

"Mom? You're home?"

"Believe it or not!" came the voice from the kitchen. Buffy's mother worked long hours at an art gallery, buying and selling valuable pieces, and often Buffy found herself at home alone. "I insisted that today I was going to do Mom things. I don't do them often enough."

Inside the kitchen, a tray of muffins sat cooling on the table. Joyce was scooping globs of mix into another muffin pan with a spoon. Buffy dropped her backpack on a kitchen chair and sat in another. She picked up a muffin, then tossed it back and forth in her hands while it cooled. Next to the tray was a stack of mail; several colorful college brochures peeked out from beneath white bill envelopes. "Okay, Mom," she said. "What's up?"

"What do you mean?"

"I know you, you know me, we're a happy fam-i-ly, so let's not tango around the kitchen. It *is* a Monday, and it *is* four-fifteen in the p.m., yet here you are."

Joyce slid the pan into the oven, then wiped her hands on her apron, which came loose with the effort. She shrugged, tossed it on the counter, and sat down beside her daughter.

"Oh, nothing really," she said. "Just wanted to touch base with you. We so rarely have time. What's new at school? Anything exciting?"

Buffy shrugged. "Two new girls, Cordy-types. And I'm Allison Gianakous's new best friend, and she wants to try out for the dead boy's place on the basketball team."

Joyce looked thoughtful. "I don't know if I think that's a good idea. Boys play more rough than girls."

Buffy raised her brows.

"Don't they?"

"You haven't been to many games of either gender recently, Mom," said Buffy. "There's very little difference. And anyway, even though I told Allison it wasn't my concern—and it's not—I don't see why Principal Snyder has such a hemorrhage over the idea. If someone is good enough, they should have a shot."

Joyce nodded. "Lots of strides have been made toward gender equality. But I guess there'll always be struggles."

"Sure."

"And speaking of female activities," said Joyce, brightening, "there's a pageant coming up in several weeks . . . you may have heard."

Buffy paused in mid-chew. *At last,* she thought. *The topic we've been heading for ever since I sat down.* "You wouldn't by any stretch mean Miss Sunnydale High?"

"Mmm-hmm," said Joyce. "As it turns out, there's going to be a mother-daughter fashion show during intermission. Businesswomen and their daughters, wearing clothes from a number of the independent clothing stores around town. The fashion show will benefit the Sunnydale Small Business Association, and is also to show Wayland Enterprises that we may welcome them, but we are strong in our own right."

"That's nice."

"And I wanted to ask you if you would agree to be in it with me?"

Buffy swallowed the bite of muffin. Oh, wouldn't Cordelia and her buddies just love to see her parading down the runway with her mother while the pageant contestants stood behind the curtain and laughed their Miss Sunnydale butts off? She took a breath, picked off another bit of muffin with her fingers, and said, "Sure, Mom, why not?"

"But . . . ," said Joyce. "Before you say yes, I just wanted to mention that your father called this afternoon. He said he's rented a cabin in the mountains the same weekend, and was hoping you'd join him for a couple days of hiking."

"Oh," said Buffy. *Uh-oh! Competing parent plans!*

"It's up to you, of course. No pressure."

"Of course not," said Buffy. *Hah!*

She finished her muffin and took her books upstairs to her bedroom. Her choice, but either way she'd be disappointing one parent. *Great.*

Buffy spent the next few hours thumbing through college brochures (the ones that had come today actually had her name right), reading over her government and physics assignments, and thinking about fashion shows and cabins. For a short while she felt almost normal, almost gloriously common. The sun went down. She turned on her bedside lamp.

A few minutes later, Joyce called Buffy for dinner. As Buffy got up from her desk, she glanced out the window and saw two vampires down on the sidewalk by her yard. They were the ones she'd fought Friday night after dinner at The Laughing Greek. They seemed to be arguing. Pulse picking up a furious pace, Buffy snatched a couple stakes from her desk drawer, and dashed down the steps and outside into the night. She scanned the darkness . . . sniffing, looking, sensing for their presence.

But they were gone.

So what was that all about?

She walked back into the house to Joyce's offering of Lean Cuisines, shaking her head and thinking that "normal" was a word she should just kick out of her vocabulary. It didn't belong there.

"And it never will," she whispered glumly.

CHAPTER 3

"I can't believe this has happened! Can you believe this has happened? It's not as if we don't have enough to worry about in this stupid little town!"

"Whining won't do any good, Viva. We need a plan."

"Before we all die!" snarled Viva.

There was a pause, as some of the vampires silently acknowledged what they thought was true, while several others, who did not believe her wild story, rolled their curdled-white eyes and shook their beastly heads.

The room was the basement of an out-of-business Beanie Baby shop on the outskirts of town; a damp cinder-block cube with ceiling-high windows that looked out on the ground-level blackness of a Sunnydale night. It was here that a group of female vampires had created a hang-out, decorated as much like The Bronze as possible— planks set atop each other on one side of the room to represent a stage, another plank on top of two stacks of cinder blocks on the other side of the room to represent the coffee and soda bar. There were no vampire bands that they knew of, and none of them could sing (that ability had pretty much gone the way of body warmth, the breath of life, and a craving for tacos), and so a boom box sat on the stage and pounded out a variety of stolen CDs by cool and obscure groups like Worm Bait and Bloody Bash. Strands of holiday lights were looped from the ceiling like electric spider webs, and small stuffed animals had been garroted within the wires, their little legs and tails hanging down. It had been Viva's idea to make a vampire-chick hangout, and though it was rare to get away from their male counterparts due to the pretty singular mindset vampires had, of getting blood and destroying the Slayer, sometimes they found it—well, relaxing in a demonish kind of way.

But not tonight. Not by a long stretch.

Viva ran her sharp nails along a bare spot of cinder block, sending blue sparks into the air. "The Olympian's time is long over," she growled. "She should know better than to come to the Hellmouth with her two brats! But here She is, trying to exert Her power once more. Our supply of humans will be poisoned again, will be made lethal to us! And all that aside, She is so disgustingly *stuck* on herself! Deadly and stuck—what a combination!"

Becky, a vampire who during her life back in the '30s in Chicago had been a very popular albino radio actress, paced back and forth, her catlike eyes glowing yellow with rage. "Okay, so what are we going to do? We can't kill them! We don't know *how* to kill them!"

"True," said Viva. "We need the Slayer, and . . ."

"Shut your mouth, Viva!" This was Barb. She was a short blond who had been a waitress in the '50s. "We aren't going to catch the Slayer. You tried Friday night and look what it got you? A coupla dusted companions. We have to get rid of the Olympian and her two maggots on our own. Just stay vigilant for the times when they come out at night."

"No, no, no!" said Viva. "You aren't hearing me! Not only can they poison our food supply, but they themselves are the most toxic to us of all. We need the Slayer! She's killed many demons and devils, and she is our only chance."

"I don't believe any of this garbage!" said the vampire Nadine. She was the oldest of them, sired in 1854 during the Civil War. She had raven black hair, and insisted on dressing in the long, billowy skirts of her time. "Viva, you've always been a big mouth, always lying about stuff. 'My mother was an heiress, my father was a duke. I would have been a famous dancer if I had stayed human.' Give me a break! You're just looking for attention."

"No, I'm not!" said Viva. "I know about Olympians! I've been with them before, and I know their power and their danger to us. If we get, say, ten of us, circle the Slayer, drag her back here, after an hour of our nails up under her nails she'll do whatever we want. Then, once the Olympians are gone, we can kill the Slayer."

"Catching the Slayer is even harder than killing her!" said Nadine. "Besides, do you think you can find ten vampires who'll believe you?" She leaned on the counter and shook her head. Her followers crossed their arms.

"Nadine may be right," said Becky. "The Slayer is too dangerous. We'll have to do this ourselves."

Viva flew into Becky's face, her twisted visage contorting even more. "We're going to starve to death!"

Becky slapped Viva down. Viva sprang back up, snarling.

"We'll think of something, Viva!" Becky screamed.

"No, we won't!"

"Yes, we will!"

"You sound like a bunch of humans!" screeched Barb. "Now just shut up. I can't concentrate on an empty stomach. We'll think better after we eat. Okay?"

Viva and Becky growled under their breath.

"Sounds like a plan to me," said Nadine.

"Okay?" Barb demanded.

The others nodded.

Barb climbed over top of the "coffee and soda" bar and opened a large wooden crate on the other side. She yanked out an old man they'd picked up down on the beach, threw him up onto the counter, and laughed as he lay there trembling, his hands and feet bound and his mouth gagged. The vampires gathered around him, rubbing their hands together.

"All right, now," Barb said. "Do you prefer your cappuccino warm or iced?"

The man screamed into the rag.

"So," said Buffy, as she, Xander, Oz, and Willow sat on the concrete bench outside school where they often met in the morning before class. "Which would you chose? A fashion show or a cabin-and-hiking weekend? Keeping in mind you'll hurt the other parent's feelings no matter what you do."

Willow shrugged. Oz said, "Male here, but I'd hike."

"Which would you choose, Xander?" asked Buffy.

"I would chose both," said Xander, his voice strangely dreamlike.

"Both?" asked Buffy. "You can't do both. It's impossible."

"Yes, I can."

"You can't do two things at the same time, remember?"

Xander blinked, shook his head and said, "What? Oh, I thought we were talking about the Moon sisters. Perfect bodies, gorgeous hair, smooth and sophisticated movements, perky faces. I like perky. I heard Polly audition for the school chorus yesterday. It was awesome! And somebody said Calli can write poetry that would melt your heart. She's already been given a position on the school literary magazine. You know, if I were a man and they were two women, I'd go for them in a heartbeat."

"Whatcha waiting for?" asked Oz. "Sic 'em, Xander. With your luck, you'll be double-dating by Saturday."

Xander rolled his eyes. With his luck, they all knew, the Moon sisters would punch him senseless with his first "Good morning."

Cordelia strolled up to the bench, her arms crossed over her books, her hair pulled back into a chic ponytail. She looked incredibly glum compared to two days ago, when she'd been leading the new girls around. She stopped at the bench and waited for someone to ask her what was wrong.

"What's wrong?" asked Willow obligingly. "You look depressed."

Cordelia tossed her ponytail. "Give them an inch and watch them take a whole foot, why don't they?" she said. She dropped down on the bench beside Buffy, squeezing in and forcing Xander to stand up. "Who do they think they are—God's gift to Sunnydale? And excuse me, but am *I* not the one who took my time to show them around, to teach them the pitfalls, to show them who and who not to ignore?"

Buffy nodded. "Yep. I remember being a pitfall."

"Right!" said Cordy. "You understand! But look at them now! How incredibly unfair and wrong is that?"

She pointed across the grassy stretch, to the curbside where the yellow and white beetles were parked. By the cars, the two Moon sisters stood among a cluster of girls and boys—for the most part Cordy's friends—and this time the sisters were carrying the conversation, while the others watched them with wide-eyed wonder. On several occasions, the sisters put their hands on someone else's shoulders, leaned in close, and laughed lightly. *Sophisticated and perky aside,* Buffy thought, *they're just a bit too touchy-cozy for me.*

"Off-kilter much?" groaned Cordelia. "So very not right much? I'm being betrayed!"

"Sorry," said Willow sympathetically.

"Yeah, tough luck," said Buffy. "Cheer up. Maybe they're just a couple of flashes in the pan."

"I don't want them to flash in the pan, don't you see?" whined Cordy. "I want to flash in the pan! It's my pan!"

"Well . . . ," said Buffy.

"Check it out," said Oz.

Allison Gianakous was being waved over by the Moon sisters, and the circle of popular kids drew in around her like mother animals around their young. Allison was tall enough that Buffy could see her face over the heads of the other students. At first she was frowning with uncertainty; then her face burst into a huge grin.

"What do they want with her?" Buffy wondered aloud.

"To tape a 'kick me' sign to her back," offered Xander.

"I hope so," said Cordelia. "For the sake of everything sacred, I sure hope so!"

The school day began as usual. Buffy stopped at her locker, then reported to Giles in the library before her first class.

Of all the rooms in Sunnydale High, the library was the most dignified, the most stately—and the most unused by the student body. Tall bookshelves lined the second floor, atop a flight of sturdy stairs, and were crammed full of volumes of many kinds, the unremarkable as well as the curious. Heavy dark wood trim set off the light walls, an old-fashioned wooden coat rack sat near the office door, and potted palms and fig plants were placed here and there, making the library look more like the private den of a well-to-do British eccentric than something in an American public school—which, in a manner of speaking, it was. The place smelled of books and intrigue.

Buffy found Giles even more irritated with Mo Moon than he had been the day before. The woman had left a memo on his desk saying she had business around town—securing Miss Sunnydale Pageant sponsorships for her two daughters—but would be back later, and that she expected to see the volumes they'd discussed in boxes and ready to be taken away.

"Cold day in hell," Giles said simply as he watered his fig plant. His hand was shaking, and the water just barely made it into the planter.

"All right, Giles," Buffy replied. "You were always one to stand on principle with words of elegance and grace."

"Don't ever doubt it," he said in a tight voice. "And how was last night's patrol?"

"Just one dusting, a lone-wolf type with one bad ear and an attitude down near the ice rink. Nothing spectacular."

"Good job," he said.

"Yeah. Hey, don't let her get you down."

"Never," said Giles, trying to smile. "Never."

Buffy tried her best to pay attention in her first few classes, but her mind kept wrangling over the camping/fashion show decision. She scribbled pros and cons for each in her notebook, but they came up equal on both sides. *Just great.*

She stopped by the restroom before lunch. She studied herself in the restroom mirror, and when nobody was looking, took several swinging, fashion-show-style steps. She could do it. She could pull off the mother-daughter thing and look fairly decent in the process, she knew it. Her mother would be appreciative. It would give Cordy a good laugh, but if that was the biggest concern, there was no concern at all.

"But what about Dad and his hiking weekend plans?" she whispered, pausing in mid-runway stride and letting her shoulders fall. "He'll be disappointed. We haven't done anything together for a long time." She slipped her backpack over her arm and took a deep breath.

"Buffy!" It was Willow, standing in the bathroom doorway, whirling her hand. "You've got to see this!"

In the hall was a student bulletin board, where clubs and other student organizations posted notices. There were homemade ads offering cars, books, computers, and CDs for sale, as well as babysitting and lawn-mowing services. And, of course, flyers announcing the upcoming Miss Sunnydale High Pageant, showing photos of the contestants and the names of their sponsors. Cordelia's sponsor was Wanda's World of Wool, "for all your knitting kneeds."

"What am I looking at?" Buffy asked Willow.

"That." Willow pointed at a long white sheet tacked to the middle of the board. It was a petition, the heading which read, "Equality in Sporting Rights—Support Allison Gianakous's right to try out for the boys' basketball team!" Someone had decorated the petition with little basketball and football stickers, and there were already seven signatures. The first one was Allison Gianakous. The second and third were Polly Moon and Calli Moon. Beneath that were four other girls' names. Cordelia's name was seventh, written in a begrudging script.

"Kind of like the old days, when people protested stuff, huh?" asked Willow.

"Kind of," said Buffy.

The sweet smell of perfume struck Buffy's nostrils before the lilting voice struck her ears. "Good afternoon!"

Buffy spun around to see the Moon sisters with Allison. The Moons wore identical sweaters and short skirts, and a new set of jewelry. Sapphire earrings. Pearl pinky rings. One wore a tear-drop diamond necklace; the other wore a choker set with three topazes. Nothing like showing off the goods. The Cordette-types would love that. The Moon sisters' long blond hair shimmered around their shoulders, and their eyes were bright and friendly. It was clear that Allison had tried to dress like them, but it was a bit off-kilter, with the skirt not quite short enough and the sweater not quite tight enough.

One of the sisters said, "If I remember correctly, you are Buffy, right?" She held out her hand as if to shake Buffy's, but she leaned her face in close as she did. Buffy stepped back, bumping into Willow. One thing she didn't like was having her personal space invaded.

"Yeah, Buffy," said Buffy, giving the girl's hand a quick squeeze and letting it go. "That's me. Tar Pit Summers! I'm sorry, you are . . . ?"

"Excuse me," said the girl with a tinkling laugh, "how impolite to expect you to remember. We really didn't get a chance to talk the other day, did we? Cordelia had us on a pretty tight schedule. I'm Calli. This is my sister,

Polly. It isn't difficult to tell Polly and me apart, as I have but the barest sprinkling of freckles on my nose, see?"

She leaned close to Buffy again, laughing and pointing at her nose. Through the strong perfume, Buffy caught a whiff of something cool, pleasant, and rose-scented in Calli's laugh. *Mouthwash?* Buffy felt light-headed for a brief moment, but she pulled away from the blond and the strange feeling dissipated.

"I see," said Buffy. "Freckles. Amazing. So, how do you like Sunnydale? Classes abysmal? Teachers depressing?"

"On the contrary! We've felt most welcome," said Polly. "Everyone has been kind and gracious. Even my mother is happy here. She enjoys her new position with the library very much. And she wants to do something for the community as well. She's thinking of starting a Women's Society of Sunnydale, her gift to the ladies here. She's always wanted to be involved in a community, but we've . . . well, we've moved so much it just hasn't been possible. Perhaps here will be the place—I do so hope that's the case!"

"So do I," said Calli.

"But," Polly's voice lowered and her mouth pursed daintily, "we do have our work cut out for us right here in this school, do we not?"

"What kind of work?" asked Willow.

"Consider the underlying conditions that have made such a thing necessary," said Calli, pointing at the petition. "Having to beg some vain male to allow girls to do what they have the free-born right to do?"

Just then a pretty, petite, brown-haired senior passing them in the hall screeched to a halt. She stared at the Moon sisters. "Somebody is speaking my language," she said, crossing her arms and raising one eyebrow. "Continue, my friend. I may like what you are saying."

Willow tugged Buffy's sleeve and the two of them exchanged glances. The brown-haired senior was Anya, a girl who wasn't really a girl at all but an eleven-hundred-year-old demon who had lost her power center and was now trapped at Sunnydale in the body of a twelfth-grader. At one time she had been an avenger of scorned women, killing unfaithful boyfriends in myriad ghastly ways. Now she was stuck in high school with no supernatural powers and an unwanted hormonal attraction to males. Xander in particular.

Calli continued. "The kind of patriarchal system we see here is archaic at best and intolerable at worst."

"Yeah!" said Allison enthusiastically. "Archaic! My word exactly! It's time we women took a stand. We've been oppressed for way too long."

"We have? Like here in Sunnydale we have?" asked Willow.

"But of course you have," said Polly. She leaned toward Willow as if she was going to tell a secret, but Willow stepped back quickly. Obviously she thought the girls were excessively chummy, too.

Polly didn't seem to notice. "Discrimination is everywhere!" she went on. "And not just in sports. In the political arena, in social situations, in economics, religion, the arts—"

"Whoa! You haven't been here very long," Buffy said sternly. "You're speaking out of turn. You don't know anything about Sunnydale, or about our school."

"But I do," said Calli. "I know that males have been in control in every age, every place, every dimension."

"Yes, so true," agreed Anya grumpily. "But nobody wants to listen to *me!*"

"Wow," said Willow. "Every dimension, huh?"

"Yes, indeed," said Polly. "And we are prepared to set things straight."

"Straight as Eros's arrow," said Calli. And to Willow, "That's a beautiful bracelet, by the way."

Polly and Calli winked their blue eyes in unison, and walked off down the hall to join several other girls near the row of lockers.

Anya shrugged and walked on. Allison remained in place, shaking with excitement. "We have to make our stand!" she said to Buffy. "Like Custer, or Billy Jack in that late-night, one-tin-soldier movie—even though he was a guy and guys are the oppressors. Do you have a pen?"

"Huh?"

"To sign the petition! You *are* going to sign? You have to sign! We have to show people like Principal Snyder and my father that we girls aren't going to take it anymore."

Buffy let out a long, silent breath. Yes, Allison had had a rough life with her dad, but was that enough of a reason to go completely rabid against all of society's males? She tugged a pen from her backpack and scribbled her name on the petition. Willow signed beneath her.

"We just did something daring!" said Willow, her voice dropping. "Besides slaying monsters, that is."

"I guess," said Buffy.

As Allison walked away to join her new popular friends, Buffy thought, *Maybe getting on the basketball team is just what she needs to get some self-esteem back. At least this is all harmless enough.*

At least it isn't going to hurt anybody.

CHAPTER 4

The next morning, Oz picked Buffy up for school in his van because it was raining, hard. Xander and Willow were in the van, too, thrilled that even though they had yet to rank wheels of their own they weren't hoofing it through the downpour. Sunnydale's streets were slick with rainwater, and some of the city's streetlights remained on because of the dark gray sky. Only one of Oz's windshield wipers was working, and it thwacked furiously back and forth against the glass, while the other one lay motionless like a broken insect leg.

"Bronzing it tomorrow night?" Oz asked, glancing over his shoulder to where Buffy and Xander were huddled in the back. "Dingoes are gonna play. We're doing a new song I wrote."

"Cool," said Buffy. "But if you don't watch the road we might not make it past the next minute."

"Oh, yeah," Oz said, looking back at the road.

"So, Xander," asked Willow. "Did you sign the petition? The one to let Allison try out for the boys' basketball team?"

"I don't see why she'd want to," Xander said. "The girls' team is better than the boys' team."

"I signed it," said Oz.

"You don't feel it's a threat to your masculinity?" asked Buffy.

"Few werewolves find their masculinity threatened."

"Good point."

The van swished to a stop in the parking lot. All four gathered their books, popped open the van doors, and dashed through the rain and into the school. Inside, everyone went their separate ways, with Buffy heading to the library to report on last night's patrolling and to see how Giles was managing with Mama Moon at the helm.

As she reached for the door handle, she heard Allison's voice in the hallway, gabbing shrilly. Buffy paused to watch a large group of girls stroll by with the Moon sisters in the front, Allison next, and at least twelve other girls—all former Cordettes—after that. Even Anya was with them, an expression of cautious uncertainty on her face. She was obviously curious enough to hang out for a while. Several stray boys tagged along at the rear for good measure, smiling like demented puppies after a plate of Beggin' Strips.

As they passed her, Calli, Polly, and Allison turned toward Buffy and in a single motion opened their cropped jackets to show her the T-shirts they were wearing underneath. The shirts had been custom designed and read, "Womyn Power!" The girls winked and went on. Allison called over her shoulder, "Unite with us, unite with us, unite with us!"

Allison's gotten way creepy, Buffy thought.

And then Cordelia was waving at Buffy from down the hall. Buffy waited, her arms crossed. This could be interesting, since Cordelia had not been part of the passing parade. Cordy was almost panting, something that was not cool to do, and she looked just a little bit disheveled—also not at all cool.

"All right, I've had it," she said to Buffy with a defiant toss of her head. "I will no longer associate with those—those freaks!"

"Freaks?"

"You heard me. They won't listen to a thing I say. They have their own little pathetic agenda, and everyone of importance seems to be agreeing with them. Everyone except me, that is. I've tried to talk to some of my friends—ex-friends—to see what's *oh-so-special* about the Moons, but they can't explain it. They like the way the Moons talk. They like the way the Moons dress. They like the way the Moons wear all that expensive jewelry regardless of how much they wear at once and how tacky it looks! They like what the Moons say. *They* like, *they* like! What about *my* likes? Since when did *my* likes become unimportant?"

"I don't know, Cordy, such a dilemma is well beyond unfathomable."

"Those two Moon girls must have some kind of supernatural power at work, and they are stealing all my friends away!"

"Cordy," Buffy said, "you're just jealous. You can't stand somebody else taking your place. If anything seems weirdly odd to me, it's Allison."

Cordelia's mouth dropped open. "I should have figured you wouldn't understand! Unless something is slobbering right in your face you just can't see it! Forget you!" She stormed off.

Buffy pushed through the library door. It eased shut behind her. "Hello?" she called.

The only sound she heard was that of a clock on the wall and her own footsteps.

"Giles?" Nothing. She walked to the base of the stairs. "You in here?"

Giles's face peeked from behind a shelf upstairs. "Hello." He looked tired. "Are you in need of anything?"

"Well," Buffy said, "nothing of critical mass. Just thought I'd stop in. Report on . . . you know." She paused and looked around. "Should I shut up? Is this bad timing?"

Giles came down the stairs with an armload of books. He dropped them into an open packing box by the checkout desk. "Bad timing? What do you mean?"

Buffy rolled her eyes, hoping he would catch on. He didn't seem to. "Is Mama Moon in here?" she whispered.

"Ms. Moon? No, she isn't. And Buffy." Giles straightened his glasses. "I shouldn't have said what I said to you the other afternoon. It was unthinking at the least and unprofessional at the worst."

"Hey, this is me," said Buffy. "We can say anything to each other. That's kind of our motto, right?"

"Yes, perhaps," said Giles. He blinked as if he were falling asleep. It made Buffy feel very uncomfortable. "So, what's on your mind?"

"Well, I'm here to report three dead vampires last night. Near the cemetery."

"Mmm, fine, fine. A dead vampire is a good vampire."

Buffy couldn't believe this. Giles was acting so disinterested, so un-Watcherlike.

"What are you doing with those?" Buffy pointed at the box. Inside were books on ancient Native American lore, several on mysterious happenings by Charles Fort, and others on Eastern European mythology and numerology. Nothing from Giles's more private collection, but books that were helpful nonetheless when it came to researching weirdnesses. "Why are you packing them up?"

"I'm taking them home," said Giles. "I've realized I've been a bit overcontrolling in my selections for the library, and Ms. Moon has had some good suggestions as to other books we could put in their places."

"You have to be kidding! These books are—"

"These books are taking up valuable space. I know such books are important to our work, Buffy. But I just think a school library might not be the best place for them."

"Earth to Giles!" Buffy took his arm. "Listen to yourself! Do you hear what you're saying?"

Giles hesitated, looking at Buffy as if he didn't know her. Then he shook his head, his eyes cleared a bit and he said, "No. What *was* I saying, Buffy?"

"That Mo Moon was right to ask you to get these books out of here."

Giles frowned. "I said that? No, that's wrong." He rubbed his temple. "I guess for a moment I thought it was a good idea. Odd."

"Odd absolutely."

"I'm sorry, Buffy. Preoccupied, I suppose, though that isn't an excuse. It won't happen again. I'll just put these back where they belong."

As Buffy helped Giles reshelf the books on the library's upper level, she said, "There are two other things I wanted to talk to you about. First, the night we both ate at The Laughing Greek. . . ."

"You *ate* there?" Giles said with a slight twinkle in his eye as he slid a book on Aleister Crowley back into place.

"The night we both *went* to The Laughing Greek," Buffy amended. "I was attacked by some female vampires not far from the restaurant, and they seemed, I don't know—to be trying not to kill me but catch me."

Giles looked concerned. "Indeed?"

"I thought I was imagining it, or that they were slow learners and hadn't quite figured out the delicate Slayer-vamp relationship. But later I saw them outside my bedroom window. I went out after them and they'd vanished. I think they're playing a game with me. I just thought I'd bring it up in case—"

"This is bad," said Giles sharply. "Why didn't you say something right away?"

"You seemed pretty caught up in your own concerns at the time. Plus I thought I had taken care of it. And even more plus, Mama Moon was just next door in your office. I just made it a brief debrief." She knew how lame this sounded.

Giles frowned. "Never leave me out of the loop, Buffy."

Buffy shook her head. "I won't. I'm sorry. Never again."

"And there was something else?"

"Yes," said Buffy. "Allison Gianakous. The way she's been acting. I never really knew her, but I've seen her around enough to know that she's not herself recently. She's always been majorly shy, and now she's loud. Obnoxious. Do you think maybe she's become possessed by the ghost of some abused female, some tormented woman's spirit who has just now decided to take a human body, manipulate high-school kids in a Southern California town to her purpose, and seek revenge by insisting she get to play boys' basketball?"

Giles's brows knitted together.

"Maybe? Sort of?"

"Buffy, I hear what you are saying . . ."

"Oooh, catchy psychoanalytic phrase."

". . . and I know Allison is normally a reserved girl. But what you are observing is only a teenager's daily stress coming to a head. There is nothing supernatural about it."

"How can you be sure? Something about the whole business makes the hairs on my arms stand up."

"Trust me on this one. This is normal. Vampires trying to kidnap you is not. It indicates a desire to use you as a bargaining chip, or make you into a slow, tortured sacrifice of some sort. You'll have to be incredibly careful, more than you usually are."

Buffy shivered. Torture. Sacrifice. Not good. "I've got a backup," she said. "I'll drop by Angel's place and ask him to—"

But Giles held up his hand. "Angel is out of town. I sent him west just last night, investigating reports of paranormal disturbances emanating from a desert cave. I believe it could be a gathering of forces that might decide to pay us a visit if we don't thwart them."

"How long will he be gone?" Buffy asked as she and Giles walked down the library steps. "How long does cave force-thwarting take?"

"I don't know. Several days. A week or more."

"And he didn't even say good-bye."

"No, well, it happens sometimes. Duty over friendship."

Friendship, thought Buffy. *How about love? She felt a pang, but pushed it down. Angel loved her. She loved him. He trusted her and she trusted him. He would have said good-bye if he'd had the chance.*

The library door opened, and Mo Moon strolled in.

She had her hair pinned neatly to her head, and she wore an impressive gray tailored suit. She smiled broadly at Buffy, said, "Well, hello there, my dear! Nice to see you again!" and went into Giles's office. Buffy noticed Giles gazing after her. His mouth had gone slack.

"Ah, is that it?" Buffy asked softly. "Is that why you were duped into packing those books? She's very pretty in a stuck-up way, but I didn't think you would let some suited-up library supervisor make you think twice about your responsibilities. About what we need in order to—"

Giles whipped around, his hand up as if he was going to slap Buffy. Buffy flinched, but did not move.

Immediately, Giles withdrew his hand and put it to his forehead. He let out a pained breath. "Buffy, that was inexcusable. I didn't mean that. I . . . I've had a very difficult week. I've not felt myself at times. Forgive me."

Buffy nodded. And then Mo Moon called from the office, "Mr. Giles, I need you!"

Giles's manner immediately shifted. He tilted his head toward Buffy and said, "Enough chatter. Go on now."

And he waved his hand toward the door, telling Buffy in no uncertain terms where to go.

Buffy dropped down onto her bed and reached for the phone. She hadn't caught Willow after school—Willow had had a dentist appointment—and Buffy needed to talk to her. She wanted to share her weird feelings about Allison. She wanted to tell Willow about Giles's change in attitude about the books in the library and about the way-not-normal attraction he had for Mo Moon.

Buffy lifted the receiver and lay back, looking at the butterflies she'd stuck all over her walls, symbols of freedom and simplicity, concepts that were completely not part of her life. *Tomorrow,* she thought, *Willow, Oz,*

Xander, and I will skip lunch and confront Giles. Have one of those intervention things. Tell him that Mama Moon's dangerous. That maybe even she has some evil force around her; you can't be too careful on the Hellmouth.

Buffy's mother was already on the line, and speaking so intently she obviously didn't hear the click.

"Hank," Joyce was saying. "This is really important to me, and this isn't something that can be changed. The date is set in stone. Your little outing isn't."

"No, it isn't, but that's not the point," came Buffy's father's voice. "You see Buffy all the time. I rarely have the chance. Why are you being so stubborn?"

"I'm not being stubborn," said Joyce. "I'm looking at the facts."

"No, you aren't," said Hank Summers. "You've got your heels dug in and you aren't budging. This is so like you, Joyce!"

"And this is so like you, Hank," said Joyce. "You're acting just like . . . like a man!"

Buffy slammed the receiver down. She didn't care if her parents knew at that moment that she had heard them arguing. It was just a stupid weekend; why couldn't they let her decide and not have major palpitations over it?

Buffy threw her book bag across the room, and it slammed into the wall. Her parents were acting just like—well, like two teenaged kids. It was crazy.

She fingered the knob on her clock radio just in time to hear the local news. Another Sunnydale High boy— Ben Rothman—had been found dead in Weatherly Park, his head stuck in a bucket full of water near the public restrooms. The police believed he drowned, likely under the influence, and they were planning an autopsy.

Not another one!

Buffy clicked off the radio and put her hand to her forehead. She remembered Brian Andrews's hopeful prejock face a few years back, looking up at her from the school-hall floor with her notebooks in his hands. "Buffy," she remembered him saying. "That's a nice name. Help me get these books."

He was sad in a kinda cute way.

"Buffy, help me get these books," he had said.

"Buffy, help me . . . !"

She blinked and looked around. That voice had sounded real. Piercing. Desperate. Was it a ghost? Or was it guilt speaking—guilt that Brian's death was something she couldn't have prevented?

"Okay," she said to herself, to Brian, and to Ben wherever they were. "I'll ask Willow to crack into the police computer files and see if there's more we should know about. Will that make you happy?"

She listened, and heard nothing.

She walked over to the window. Late-afternoon shadows swirled around the trees and lawn. She could see a row of yellow roses her mother had tried to stake up along the yard's edge. They were tilted at extreme angles, but were there, nonetheless. This was her mother's attempt at a normal, domestic activity, kind of like baking muffins, to perhaps prove that yes, this was a normal family living here. Buffy let out a breath and wondered, once more, why she was the Chosen One. Why she was responsible for stopping evil. Why she just couldn't take a vacation.

She looked at the butterflies on her wall. "Unlike you guys, I don't have a lot of free time in my life."

Then she picked up the phone, found a dial tone, and called Willow.

CHAPTER 5

The school was buzzing the next morning. Word was out that not only had Allison taken her petition to the boys' basketball coach to demand to try out, but junior Ashley Malcolm was already insisting she have a go at Ben Rothman's empty spot on the wrestling team.

Buffy sat at her desk in her first class, awaiting announcements and mentally preparing for the talk she and her friends would have with Giles during lunch. Willow had returned her call late the night before, having hacked into the Sunnydale Police Station computer system. The reports on Brian and Ben were still incomplete and basically useless. *But we can still do something about No Moon.*

Suddenly, several boys in the back of the room got into a heated discussion with several girls.

"I don't get it," said Justin Shifflett. "Someone needs to knock Allison and Ashley down a couple pegs! They don't belong on the boys' teams any more than a pig belongs in a ballet."

"Think they'll show you guys up?" demanded Piper Reynolds. "Afraid they'll do better than the boys?"

"That's not the point," said Raul Mendez. "It's an invasion! Ben Rothman hasn't even been dead twenty-four hours and Ashley wants his wrestling position? It's those Moon sisters. They're the instigators!"

"That *is* the point!" said Piper. "You're scared!"

"Am not!"

"Are, too!"

"Am not!"

Buffy whirled around in her seat. "You sound like third-graders! Next thing you know, you'll each be claiming the other one has cooties!"

The students stopped, stared at her, and in unison the girls said, "Will not!"

The boys glared at the girls. "Will, too!"

The teacher tapped her desk with her pen and said, "Principal Snyder has asked me to read something to you. He asks that you take it seriously."

The students slowly took their seats and stared at the teacher. The woman held up the paper.

"To the student body of Sunnydale High School: It has come to my attention that there is a divisive argument brewing on our campus. It will stop immediately. The argument concerns sports team tryouts. Let me make this clear: No girl will be allowed to try out for any empty place on a boys' sports team. This is not an arbitrary decision, but a rule that has been in place ever since the opening of the school. Boys will do boys' sports. Girls will do girls' sports. This is not discrimination. It is common sense. Many events are cross-gendered. But athletics must and will remain separated."

Piper and several other girls stood up and angrily stormed out of the room, in spite of the teacher's demands that they return to their seats. Justin, Raul, and a couple of boys shook their heads. "Female emotional-ism," whispered Justin snidely. "They can't help it. An-other reason they should stay off our teams."

The bell rang, and students flooded the halls. Buffy went to her locker, then stopped by the girls' restroom to wash some ink from a leaky pen off her hands. After she'd rinsed, she discovered there were no paper towels in the dispenser. But toilet paper was paper.

As she was in a stall, unrolling a wad and wiping it across her fingers, she heard voices and footsteps com-ing into the restroom.

The Moon sisters.

Buffy eased the stall door shut, flipped down the toilet lid and crouched there, wondering if she was being paranoid. Why didn't she want to see these girls? Well . . . aside from the fact that they were clutchy-grabby and their mother was spooky.

"The scene in my first class was quite delectable. I don't believe the reaction could have been any more ap-propriate." The voice was that of Calli Moon. "The girls were rightly offended by Principal Snyder's announce-ment, and the boys were outraged. They showed their silly masculine emotionalism in front of everyone."

Polly continued, "Principal Snyder's words revealed nothing more than a male lashing out at something he is unable to control or stop. Well, I say bring on the chal-lenge and it shall be rightly met!"

The next voice was Allison's. "Oh yeah?" she screeched. "Oh, yeah? No kidding, girlfriend!"

A gentle, corrective voice—"Allison, try again, please."

Allison lowered her voice. "Sorry. I mean, I do believe you are correct, Calli."

Now she's trying to talk like the Moons, thought

Buffy. *That's kinda creepier than the way she* was *talking.*

"It is such a fine thing that your family came to Sunnydale," Allison continued slowly, haltingly, thinking her words before she said them. "We are truly blessed by your presence."

Buffy leaned against the steel wall and peered through the crack by the door. She saw Allison, Calli, and Polly, looking in the mirrors and readjusting their jewelry.

"You are our dearest Number Three," said Polly, giving Allison a hug. "And you're doing such an excellent job, promoting the ideals, spreading the word! We are so proud."

"Oh, I should say so," chimed in Calli. "We are proud of you. And that is a lovely ring. Is it amethyst?"

Allison held it up. "Yes. I've never worn it to school. My father wouldn't let me. It was my mother's."

"I would like that," said Calli simply.

And just as simply, Allison slid it off and handed it to Calli. Calli slipped it on her finger and gazed at it lovingly. "Beautiful," she said, her voice hushed with rapture. "Absolutely exquisite."

The bathroom door banged open and several other girls came in. Buffy pressed her nose closer to the crack to see two girls, whom she thought were sophomores, gather at a mirror with makeup in hand. This close to the crack, Buffy could smell the Moons' perfume, and the strength of it nearly made her sneeze. She pinched her nose.

The sophomores gave the Moon sisters a sideways, withering glare. As one whipped her mascara tube from her purse, she said, "So, you're the girls who hate boys. You are totally messed up."

"Yeah," said another sophomore. "Messed up majorly bad."

But the Moons didn't flinch or rise to their own defense. Instead, they came close to the sophomores, smiling their calm smiles, and put their hands on the girls' shoulders. The girls stared in disbelief. The Moons leaned in very, very close.

"My sweet child, you just don't understand," said Polly, "but I think you will if you just give it time. Do you know what it is to be female?"

"Sure," said one sophomore nervously. "I'm not stupid."

"It is creative power," said Polly.

"It is physical power," said Calli.

"And spiritual power," said Polly. "All that and more. Don't let your silly little boyfriends take that from you. Don't let them treat you as if you were less than they."

"Or even equal. We're superior," said Calli. "Trust us."

"Trust us," said Polly.

The girls had backed into the sinks but had no farther to go, and by the time the Moon sisters had finished talking, their demeanors had changed. They were no longer frowning, but were smiling with what seemed to be awe and revelation. They put their makeup back into their purses, then followed Polly and Allison out of the bathroom. Calli let the others go around her and out, then called back, "Don't forget to flush, Buffy!"

Buffy counted to ten, then came out of the stall. The bathroom still smelled of perfume, and the Moon sisters' words still echoed on the tiles of the walls.

Trust us. Trust us.

And then another voice spoke deep in Buffy's ear, buzzing like an insect. *"Buffy, help me . . . !"*

Buffy's heart kicked against her ribs. She looked at the mirror, expecting to see someone staring at her.

There was no one. "Who are you?" she whispered. "How do I help you?"

"Buffy!"

"Brian Andrews, is that you?"

"No, it's not Brian, it's me," came an irritated feminine voice from the stall by the window. "Can't you tell the women from the men anymore? Way sad, Buffy. Way, way pathetic."

"Cordy?"

The stall door opened and Cordelia came out. She peered cautiously around, then straightened her shoulders.

"Why were you hiding?" asked Buffy.

"Same reason you were," said Cordelia. She went to the mirror, checked her hair, and reapplied her lipstick. "The Moons are demons. Dreadful, dorkish demon debutantes. You know that as well as I do."

"Cordelia—"

Cordy wheeled about, jabbing her lipstick at Buffy like a sword. A stubby, tiny, cylindrical sword with a soft, pink tip. "Nobody in this school believes that there is anything wrong with the Moons. Somebody has to, and that somebody has to be you!"

"If you'd–"

"You're the only one who can do anything about it! You saw the way the Moons got in those girls' faces, and the way the girls changed. Don't pretend you didn't!"

Buffy held up her hand. "Cordy, listen to me—"

"Just get rid of them! They're using mind control! They're taking people's jewelry by just asking! But the really worst part of it all? They might sabotage the pageant and make me lose! Who knows what they're really up to?"

"Cordy . . . !"

"Buffy," said Cordelia. "You thought a ghost was calling your name a minute ago. And right after the Moons had been in here. Do you think that's a coincidence?"

Four seniors bounced through the restroom door, laughing about a trigonometry quiz they'd just failed. Buffy grimaced at them. Then, quietly she said, "Cordy, I've been trying to tell you that I believe you might have something, okay? I'll watch them. Slayerette-mode, sharp, vigilant. All that. But would you want to do something really productive right now? If so, come with us to talk to Giles during lunch. He's—"

But Cordelia cut her off. "During lunch? Oh, no way. An absolute nope. The girls in the pageant are having a meeting. To discuss our talents and what kind of lighting we'll need to make us look our best. It doesn't *get* much more productive than that."

During the rest of her morning classes, Buffy's brain was running full tilt, turning over and over the peculiar occurrences of the past days. Allison's rise to popularity and change of personality. The growing rift between the girls and boys at school. The drowning deaths of two high-school boys. Giles's changing attitude toward the contents of the school library, and his attraction to the supervisor.

And the powerful influence the Moon sisters had over other kids.

Buffy mustered the forces at lunch.

"With some luck this can be short and sweet," she told Willow, Oz, and Xander in the hall, as other students pressed past them and into the cafeteria. "Giles seems really into the library supervisor, while just days ago he couldn't stand the sight of her. He's getting forgetful and, I hate to say it, careless. I think Mama Moon is bad mojo. Intervention is the only way. Intervene him right out of his fantasy and into the real world."

"And this sure is the real world I'd want to trade *my* fantasies for," said Xander with a roll of his eyes.

Buffy went on. "She has a matronizing attitude, a really bad dislike of good books, and two daughters I don't trust. We have to snap Giles out of his daze. We'll need his help."

Willow raised her brows and said, "Then let's do it! Giles can't ignore the power of four! Hey, that's a rhyme!"

But the library was locked. The day was only half over, and the hallowed sanctuary of book-type learning was shut up tight. Willow, Xander, Oz, and Buffy all took turns trying to pull it open.

Oz pounded on the door, then shook his head. "Nobody's home," he said.

"The library is never closed in the middle of the day," said Willow. "Maybe Giles went home sick?"

"Or maybe he's avoiding us," said Buffy.

"That's so unlike him," said Willow.

Buffy glanced left and right, and then with one swift blow of her foot, kicked the door, breaking the lock. The door swung open.

"Remind me to remind you to say something before you do that again," said Xander. "My hand was *this* close to the door handle!"

The four stepped inside the library.

"Giles?" called Willow. "Hello?"

It was obvious to Buffy with one glance. The bookshelves on the upper level were less crowded than they had been before. Although other students wouldn't have caught it, to the Slayer it was blatant. Giles had been at it again. Cleaning house.

"What in the name of the gods is going on?" It was a woman's voice behind them. Buffy looked over her shoulder to see Mo Moon standing in the doorway, frowning and holding a stack of fliers.

"Oh, hi," said Buffy. She felt Willow, Xander, and Oz at a loss for words. Not that Oz had ever been the type with many words to share as it was, but if he had been, he'd have been at a loss, too.

"The library door was locked," said Ms. Moon. She spoke with a cool calmness that slid over Buffy's skin like sandpaper. She did so very much not like this woman. "How did you get in? Is that a broken lock I see?"

"Foot spasm," said Buffy. "Reflex. It's a trauma reaction I have to locked doors. It reminds me of when I was a little girl and my wicked godmother locked me in the crawl space under our house when I was bad."

"She couldn't help it, kicking the door," said Willow. "She has terrible memories. Spiders. Ugh! And centipedes."

"And moldy, forgotten stuffed animals with spooky little eyes," added Xander.

Mo said, "Is there anything I can do for you?"

"About the spasm?" asked Buffy.

"About books. Why you might be in the library."

"We were looking for Giles," said Xander. "Did you lock him in here?"

Buffy cut him a sharp glance.

But Mo began to smile. Then she laughed, a tinkling laugh like that of her daughters. "Such jokesters! I do love a sense of humor! No, Giles isn't here. He took the rest of the day off. I asked him to visit the middle-school library, to see what kinds of literature they provide for *their* students."

"Oh," said Buffy. "He didn't mention to me that he was going to take half a day off."

"Should he? I'm the supervisor. He reports to me. Should he also report to the students?"

As Buffy and the others turned to leave, Mo blocked them with a handful of fliers. The large print at the top read "Women's Society of Sunnydale."

"I'd like you to pass those out in your neighborhoods," said Mo. "Buffy, I believe your mother works in the arts? This would be just the organization for her. It promotes cultural awareness, history, aesthetics—oh, the lot. Would you students do that for me?"

"Sure," said Willow. "No prob. Uh, thank you."

The four went outside for the rest of lunch period. Buffy trashed her fliers in the nearest can. Oz and Xander did the same. "But," began Willow, "we said we'd—"

Buffy shook her head in disbelief. Willow slowly added her fliers to those in the trash can.

Then Xander said, "Giles sure didn't get very far." Buffy, Oz, and Willow looked out to the teachers' parking lot. Giles's car was still parked there, and he was sitting at the wheel.

Buffy reached the car first. She opened the driver's door and said, "Hey, Giles, what's up?"

Giles looked over at her, his brows drawn in confusion. "I . . . I don't know exactly. I was supposed to go somewhere, but I forgot where."

"The middle-school library," said Xander.

"Yes, yes," said Giles. "That was it. I couldn't remember." He laughed uncertainly. "I wonder how long I've been sitting here? Looking much like an idiot, I imagine."

Buffy, Oz, Xander, and Willow all climbed into the

car with Giles. Buffy sat in front. The others sat in the back, leaning forward, smashed against each other.

"What is this?" asked Giles, sounding more Giles-like. "Did I promise to drop you off at the mall or something?"

"This is an intervention," said Buffy. "So don't try to get out of the car or I'll throw you back in." It sounded mean. She didn't mean it to sound mean but it did. *Tough.*

"Intervention? I'm sorry but . . . ," began Giles.

"You have to keep your distance from Mama Moon," said Buffy. "I don't know exactly what her problem is, but she is no good for Sunnydale High. You know that, or you seem to, until she comes around and you get all . . ."

"Goo-goo eyes," said Xander.

"I do not!" said Giles.

"You do," said Buffy. "I've seen it. Giles, she has some kind of power over you. Don't let her trick you into stripping all the important things from the library. We're talking the safety of Sunnydale here. You know that! And remember the 'Secret Agent' song from my mother's oldies station. 'A pretty face can hide an evil mind.' We need you. Keep your distance."

"Keep your distance," said Oz.

"Keep your distance," said Xander.

"Keep your distance," said Willow. "Please?"

Giles took a deep breath. There was a long pause. Then he said, "So—this is an intervention?"

All four students nodded.

Giles smiled with one side of his mouth. "Interesting concept. Regardless, I appreciate your effort. I won't let my . . . I'll be vigilant and observant around Mo Moon. She does seem to have a certain influence, I know."

"Thank you." Everyone got out of the car except Giles.

"Have a good weekend," Buffy bid him as he drove off. "And get some sleep. You look exhausted."

Dingoes Ate My Baby had a gig at The Bronze that night, and as usual, they packed in a crowd. The Bronze was a popular night spot for teens and young adults. At first glance it seemed rather skeezy, but it was just rough enough, just loud enough, and just cool enough to draw in everyone from the most popular to the most not. Buffy remembered her first time here, feeling alone, friendless, and all-around uncomfortable, strolling amid the music and the pinging pinball machines and a noisy game going on at the red-covered pool table, watching for someone, anyone, with whom to talk and make that first connection. But here she had forged a friendship with Willow and Xander, and here she had spent many relaxed evenings.

As relaxed as an evening could get for a Slayer, that is.

"It might be pheromones," said Buffy as she sat at a small table with Willow and Xander. Oz was warming up with the group on the other side of the huge, crowded room.

"What might be?" asked Willow, who'd been drinking a mocha cooler and had paused in mid-sip. Her straw was stuck to her lip.

"Mo Moon's not the only Moon with personal power. Polly and Calli seem to have it, too. Cordelia says they're demons. That might be a little extreme, but she's right about the power thing." Buffy nodded in the direction of the Moon sisters and their followers, near the stage. The two sisters stuck out of the crowd like two brilliant stars in a night sky—all shimmering hair and glittering jewels. "I've been watching them for nearly an hour. Completely creepy."

"*Cordy* is right? Like she figured out something before us?" asked Xander.

"It's getting her where she lives," said Buffy. "Popularity. The pageant. All that Cordelia stuff. So she's tuned in to them on a really high frequency."

Willow shrugged. "Maybe the Moon girls have gotten a large group of friends because what they say makes sense."

"Oh?" said Xander. "You agree? 'Women good, men bad'?"

"It's not that simple."

"Sure it is," said Xander. "Men suck, women walk on water. That's just about it in a nutshell."

"Xander . . ."

Buffy put her hands on their arms. "Wait. Listen to me. Forget what their agenda might be for a minute. They're more than our usual disgustingly alert and bright new students. Like mother, like daughters. Why not? Our mothers teach us to style our hair. Maybe Mo teaches her daughters another skill entirely."

"Think so?" asked Willow. "Wow."

Buffy took a sip of her latte. "Yes. And I need you to help me do some research on the effects of scents on behavior. I suspect some kind of pheromone is in their perfume."

Willow nodded. "Sure, Buff. No problem. Monday in the library, first thing."

A shriek cut through the air, and everyone stopped talking at the same moment to turn and see what the commotion was.

Several more shouts came, the words unintelligible

but buzzing with emotion. Buffy hopped up onto her chair and stared. A large chunk of The Bronze's population was heading for the door. It looked like the two sisters were in the lead.

"What's that all about?" asked Xander.

"I can't tell," said Buffy.

She pushed through the crowd, with Willow and Xander behind her. They made their way outside.

Standing on the gravel in the pale light that pooled from The Bronze's open door, two factions had split apart. One group was seething with anger, wagging fingers at the other group. The second group, however, was smiling with nerve-grating calmness.

The group of smilers was headed by Polly and Calli Moon. Among their clan were Allison, Ashley Malcolm, a slew of elite girls, the sophomores from the bathroom, some other girls Buffy didn't know except by sight, as well as a handful of boys who looked dazed and befuddled.

Cordelia was against the outer wall, watching in horror.

"Cordy." Buffy went over to her. "What's happening?"

Cordelia's lips rolled grimly in between her teeth. This scene was clearly killing her. Here she stood, watching a battle she never in a million years would have approved of—a battle of the sexes. She liked boys. She *loved* boys. They were to be used, of course, and manipulated and taken advantage of. But not treated like aliens. Not excluded from day-to-day living. How much fun was *that?*

"I don't know," was all she said to Buffy. "Ask them."

"We aren't concerned by your concern," Calli was saying, her voice raised like that of a politician running for office. "It is not even an issue. You will come to understand our point of view, we have no doubt. Every last one of you. But until then, we will carry on our social activities elsewhere. It's clear we aren't wanted here. Yet." With a flash of her "Womyn Power" T-shirt, and subsequent flashing of everyone else's T-shirts, they turned and strolled off down the narrow alleyway and into the darkness. Those who had challenged them watched after them, grumbling and swearing.

Anya brushed past Cordelia and Buffy. "Aren't you two coming? It's really worth listening to, even if they are lowly mortals. Maybe I can convince them to take up the cause of some dumped girlfriends, bash a few masculine brains in on their behalf. It sure would lift my spirits a bit. God, I miss the old days!"

"You go on ahead," said Buffy.

Polly Moon came back through the group and instructed the boys who had been with them to stay at The Bronze. They obediently stopped, looked at each other and then the ground, and said nothing. Then Polly tossed her blond hair, came to stand in front of Willow, and with a huge smile and a finger twisting her bright diamond necklace said, "Willow Rosenberg, we're going to have a party tonight at The Laughing Greek. Allison says we can use it as our new hangout, since we aren't wanted here anymore. We really would like you to come. Please?"

"Me?" asked Willow.

"Yes," said Polly. She grinned again, wider.

"Well . . ." Buffy could see Willow struggling. "I'm not exactly somebody who is going to try out for a boys' sports team. I don't even play girls' stuff very well."

"We celebrate all talents," said Polly. "Athletic, musical, artistic, intellectual. All that it is to be feminine. We really admire your brain, Willow."

"You do?" Willow sounded hopeful.

Xander said, "Forget them, Willow, you have us."

Willow hesitated, then said, "No, thanks, I think I'll stay here with my friends."

"Certainly, Willow," said Polly. "But know that we'd love to have you with us! Keep that in mind, all right?" With a wink of her eye, she ran off to join the others.

Willow stared after the retreating Womyn. Something was brewing in her mind, Buffy could see it. Then Willow said, "You know, Buffy. I could be a spy. I could go with them and observe what they do and what they say up close. It would be more fun than library research—I'm not saying I won't help you look stuff up, but this would be firsthand. Official."

"I'm not sure that's a good idea."

"If I start feeling woozy from the perfume I'll leave right away. And besides, if need be, I can conjure up a spell to protect myself! I'm a witch, don't forget! They invited me, they won't suspect I'm watching their every move!"

"Willow . . ."

Willow's face fell. "You don't trust me to be a spy? I'm just an old reliable computer nerd?"

"No, of course not, Willow. You're smart in a lot of ways."

"Okay, then," said Willow. "I'm going. I'll check in with you tomorrow. And don't worry, Mom! I'll be fine! Just call me Ninety-nine!"

Willow took off down the alleyway, vanishing the way of the Womyn.

"Ninety-nine?" asked Buffy.

Xander shrugged sheepishly. "Back in elementary school I used to coerce her into watching reruns with me in exchange for me playing doctor with her. Real doctor, I mean. I was the patient—I had to listen to her read medical texts out loud."

Buffy and Xander went back inside and listened to most of the Dingoes set, then left The Bronze during the last song. Neither wanted to be there when the band finished, leaving them to explain to Oz that Willow preferred to play spy rather than hear her boyfriend's new music.

They strolled silently for a few minutes. As they turned a corner and started down a deserted street, Xander said, "Think Willow will be okay?"

"I hope so. She's smart. She's got good sense. But she isn't a very good witch. Well, she *is* a good witch in that she's not bad like the Witch of the West, but she's not really a good witch because she isn't very practiced."

"Did you just make sense?"

"I don't know. Did I?"

Then she stopped and sniffed the air. Her blood began to buzz in her veins. She stopped. Xander stopped.

"Shhhh," she warned him.

"Oh, great," he muttered. "Vampires, right?"

It was indeed vampires. Slithering down the rough brick wall of the warehouse by the street came two vampires, growling low in their throats. Their eyes sparkled like flint being struck, winking an obscene and mesmerizing rhythm. They reached the ground and hopped upright with lithe agility, then one tugged a large mesh net from inside her billowy coat and tossed one end to her companion. They grinned and waved the net, like two demonic fishermen out for a batch of cod.

Buffy recognized the vampires as the two who had

been outside her house, the same two who had confront-
ed her the night of the dreadful Laughing Greek dinner.
The net was unsettling; she could not let them snare her
or it would be incredibly hard to escape.

"Viva!" said Buffy as she tugged three sharp stakes
from her backpack and shook them. "We meet again!
Why only two tonight? Are the others back home afraid
of a little dusting?"

Xander pulled a cross from his shirt pocket and held it
out. "What's the deal with the net?" he whispered.

"They have some way ridiculous idea that they want
to capture me instead of kill me," Buffy whispered back.
"Maybe they're on a scavenger hunt and I'm worth a
hundred points."

Xander brightened. "I wonder how much I'm worth?"

Buffy gave him a quick, tight glance and he clutched
the cross more tightly. It shook in his grip.

With her free hand, Viva uncoiled a long, heavy chain
from her waist and snapped it at Buffy's head. Buffy
jumped aside and it hit Xander on the shoulder, tearing
his jacket and cutting through to the flesh. "Ow!" he
wailed, nearly dropping his cross.

Viva glowered and hissed. With a rapid side step, she
lunged closer to Buffy and threw the chain again, aiming
for the Slayer's neck. Buffy jumped and twisted aside,
but it caught her around the waist, pinning one arm to
her side. She fell to the ground with an "umph!", biting
her tongue and nearly dropping the stakes.

"Buffy!" yelled Xander.

Both vampires squealed in delight, and with a lightning-
quick flip of their wrists hurled two loose ends of the net
toward their prey. But Buffy tossed a stake with her un-
pinned hand, and it caught Viva's partner square in the
chest. The vampire fell backward and exploded like a

smoke bomb. Viva growled. Xander dove toward the falling net and tangled himself in it before it could land on Buffy. He slammed into the ground and rolled, wrapping himself like a cocoon. For the barest second Viva looked between Xander in the net and Buffy in the chain, then dove toward Buffy with her gnarly, slashing fingers curled with vicious intent.

Buffy struggled against the chain, trying to wriggle free. The other two stakes were in her pinned hand and she did not have enough moving room to throw them or even turn them up in Viva's direction. And then Viva landed on her, and Buffy could smell the foul breath and feel the cold flesh. She flipped, taking the surprisingly heavy Viva over, and now she was on top of the vampire, shaking as hard as she could, feeling the chain begin to loosen. "Xander!" she called. "Get over here! I need your help!"

"I'm kinda tied up at the moment!"

Viva struggled beneath Buffy, twisting her head and body, stinking spit flying from her lips and into Buffy's face. Then Buffy sat bolt upright and dumped the chains off, but Viva kneed her in the gut and sprang up and away. Buffy caught her breath, leaped to her feet, and aimed a stake at the vampire.

Suddenly there was a shout from behind Viva, and Buffy could see two male vampires running in their direction. Viva heard them, too, and glanced over her shoulder with what Buffy could only interpret as extreme irritation.

"I can handle this!" Viva shouted. "Get out of here!"

The male vampires skidded to a stop and looked at her with confused amazement. "Handle what?" said one with a mangy flattop. "We're gonna help you slay the Slayer!"

"No!" said Viva. "I need to catch her!"

Buffy slowed to listen.

The other male laughed. "No way, Viva! She kills us, we kill her, it's been that way since the dawn of time."

"Shut up and listen," said Viva. "It's the Moons, we need her to stop the Moons!"

Why is a vampire worried about the Moon family? Buffy wondered.

"Yeah, yeah," said the flattop. "We've heard rumors about your crazy idea. Nobody believes you, Viva."

"You'd best!" Viva wailed. "I know what I'm talking about, I've seen it firsthand. . . ."

Buffy hadn't seen a good vampire spat in a long time. But enough was enough. She flung one of her remaining stakes at the gathering. Flattop caught it in his ribs and dusted immediately. The other male ran for her, but she ducked and kicked out with a high, powerful thrust that drove into his jaw. He was knocked to his hands and knees, snapping and snarling. Viva screamed, "The net, damn it!"

Buffy slammed her last stake clear through the back of the male vampire and out the other side, then drew it back out deftly. Viva wailed as he evaporated into dust.

Buffy straightened and turned toward Viva, thinking, *Now I subdue her, force the truth about the Moons from her, then kill her!* But the female vampire had vanished. Buffy looked up and down the narrow, dark street, but Viva was gone—yet again.

"Hey," came Xander's voice.

Buffy looked over to see him still as tightly bound as ever, his eyes wide, the cross still at his chest as if he were a penitent monk performing some bizarre form of self-discipline. She rolled him out of the net and helped him to his feet. He shook his head, dizzy, and said, "Thanks, Buff. Where would I be without you?"

"Probably not killing vampires, that's where."

And as they dusted themselves off and Buffy replaced the stakes in her backpack, she thought, *Why would a vampire fear common mortals like the Moons? Unless like the Moons they're not mortals after all?*

CHAPTER 6

As soon as she got home, she tried to call Willow. Joyce was working late, and she had the house to herself. With a couple of left over lemon-poppyseed muffins in hand, she sat on the top of the kitchen table, dialed her friend's number, and listened to the rings.

She and Xander had gone by The Laughing Greek after the vampire attack, but no one had been there. Short party. Maybe a bust. Buffy hoped so. Even though it was late, she wanted to call and make sure her friend was all right.

Willow answered on the fourth ring, right before her machine would have picked up. "Yes, hello?"

"Willow, hey. How was the party at The Laughing Greek?"

"Wow, you don't miss a beat. I got home just about fifteen minutes ago."

"Oh," said Buffy. Willow *sounded* the same. Maybe she was okay after all. But she asked, "How was it? What happened? Who was there? Do you feel okay?

Dizzy? Groggy? Nauseous? Did you have to perform a self-saving ritual?"

"Buffy, you sound like a cop. 'Just the facts, ma'am!' "

"I don't mean to, but I need to know. You were with the Moon sisters in close proximity. And . . . ?"

"And what?"

"Like I said? Do you feel like yourself?"

Willow laughed her soft, raspy laugh. Yes, it really *did* sound like the regular old Willow. "Buffy, it was fine, honest. I didn't become the center of attention or anything, 'cause this is *me* we're talking about, but it was a good group of girls. They're very enthusiastic about Ashley and Allison and the tryouts, and other things, too. Like bathroom mirrors and things."

"Bathroom mirrors?"

"Oh, you know, like when our bathrooms are really crowded with everybody checking their hair and makeup and there isn't anybody in the boys' bathroom, they think we should be allowed to go in and use their mirrors."

"I don't know about that. . . ."

"Well, it's something to think about, isn't it? But I didn't notice anything odd, okay? They aren't using mind control. They aren't demons. I'm fine. Allison is fine. Calli and Polly are fine. Trust me."

"I had a run-in with a vampire tonight who seemed very frightened of the Moon family for some reason."

Willow chuckled again. "Maybe the vamp's just envious. The Moons are pretty and talented. Most vampires aren't."

Buffy let out a long, silent breath. Then she said, "I don't know. The vampire's interest seemed peculiar."

"Vampires are peculiar by nature, Buffy," Willow said, imitating Giles.

"Hey, tomorrow's Saturday," said Buffy. "Let's stop by Giles's and tell him about the vampire and your spy gig, and then do a little shopping."

"Oh, I'm sorry, I can't. I have stuff to do."

"Really? More important stuff than that? Like what?"

"Oh, stuff. Sorry."

"Then Sunday afternoon. Let's go Sunday."

"I can't. I'm going to enter the pageant. I have to figure out my clothes, my talent, that kind of thing. Then Sunday night we're all meeting at the restaurant to practice our pageant stuff, whatever that is, but it sounds cool, doesn't it? There is so much to think about, Buffy. And not much time to do it!"

"Willow, the pageant . . . ?"

"Good night, Buff. See you Monday!"

"Willow . . ."

The phone went dead in Buffy's hand. "Good night, Willow," she said.

Buffy went by Giles's condo Saturday morning for a training session. She wore a T-shirt and a pair of spandex biker's shorts. Her hair was tied up in a ponytail.

Giles moved the furniture back in his living room, and they sparred with chains and a net. Only one picture frame was broken in the process.

When they had finished, Giles commended her on the care she'd taken with the vampires the previous evening. "But I am going to get in touch with Angel and hasten him along. I want you to have someone here who can investigate any kidnapping plan from the inside. Unless you can kill this female."

"I want Angel back," said Buffy, wiping sweat from her brow with a towel Giles had handed her. "But I'm going to find out what she wants and what she knows, then kill her. No problem."

Then she said, "Willow spent part of the evening with the Moon sisters last night. She went to spy on them."

"Why?" Giles poured himself a cup of tea and tipped his head, indicating he could pour one for Buffy, too. She shook her head.

"Because there is something happening there. Supernatural or natural—I don't know. But they are exerting control over a lot of kids. The girls who hang with them have gotten rude and unnecessarily aggressive. The boys who hang with them are acting pretty much nonexistent."

"Buffy," said Giles. "I told you not to waste your time worrying about some here-today, gone-tomorrow high-school clique. If your attention is divided, then it will be less than optimal. You must remain sharp."

The phone rang. Giles caught the receiver. "Yes, hello?" His face softened, and his voice did as well. "Good morning to you, too. Yes, nice to hear from you. A moment, please?" He looked over at Buffy. "Are we done for now?"

"Sure," said Buffy. She walked to the door, began to call good-bye, but he sounded too happy to be disturbed. *Maybe it's an old friend from England,* she thought as she went outside and pulled the door closed. *Maybe it's a relative.*

Or maybe it's Mo Moon.

"No, he promised," she told herself, squinting in the sun until she was able to get her shades in place. "And Giles doesn't break promises."

The rest of Saturday was spent studying for government, narrowing college brochures into two piles—cool-looking places and places she wouldn't be caught dead at—and patrolling in the evening for vampires, which turned up nothing but a false alarm when a collie jumped over a fence and knocked her down over on Pine Avenue.

Sunday she shopped for groceries with her mother, then helped Joyce organize her tax materials. Joyce had a dinner meeting with the Small Business Association, so Buffy made herself a sandwich and ate it alone in the kitchen. At sunset she shouldered her weapon bag and went out for her nightly patrol.

Willow had mentioned a get-together at The Laughing Greek tonight. A prepageant meeting of some sort. Buffy didn't know exactly what she'd find, but curiosity drove her feet in that direction.

Like the Moon sisters, the restaurant was detectable by smell well before she was close to it—a stench of burned bread, some sort of horrendous cheese concoction, and a blend of spices that turned Buffy's stomach. Buffy's nose was twitching uncomfortably a whole half-block away. Mr. Gianakous clearly had not gotten any better at cooking.

But his establishment had become a hit.

Music was playing inside, and she could hear loud, chattering voices. Buffy pressed her face to the front window and peered inside. She saw that Mr. Gianakous had renovated the banquet room, knocking out a wall and making it possible for the whole Moon clique to gather together here. And the clique was there in full force. Including Allison and Ashley and Mama Moon herself.

Buffy knelt down so she wouldn't be spotted, the knee of her pants coming down on a piece of chewing gum on the sidewalk. She grimaced, but then squinted her eyes, looking deeper through the glass and into the restaurant. She crossed her fingers in hopes that Willow would not be there. Willow didn't need this nonsense. But there she was, laughing, chatting, even joining the group in a song—or was it a chant?—that Polly began to lead with a surprisingly beautiful singing voice. Buffy had all sorts of powers, but reading lips wasn't one of them, so she had no idea what the words to the song were.

But through the warped glass of The Laughing Greek it sounded like "yeeee-ahhh, weeee-ahhh, yeeee-ahhhh, ho!"

It sounded like laughter. Like melodic, evil laughter.

Willow was wearing a "Womyn Power" T-shirt Monday at school. She caught up with Buffy at her locker and proudly displayed her new chick-wear.

"Do you love it?" she asked enthusiastically, spinning around. "Isn't it great? I feel all, I don't know, special!"

Buffy took Willow by the arm. "You *are* special, Willow. You don't need a bunch of . . . of whatever they are, telling you what to wear."

"But they aren't telling me what to wear," said Willow, her face darkening. "I want to wear this. Aren't you happy that finally the popular girls accept me? How unfair!"

"That's not it at all. I don't like the Moons, and we can't get any closer until we know what we're dealing with."

"You don't know what you're talking about."

"But I do. I watched you guys through the window last night. Chanting? Swaying? What kind of pageant warmup is that? I got a bad feeling all the way through the glass."

Willow wasn't upset that Buffy had peeked in on

the meeting. In fact, she chuckled. "You don't really know anything until you try it, Buff. We'd love to have you!"

"Hey!" It was Oz, coming down the hall in their direction. He hadn't shaved in two days; the stubble looked ruggedly cool.

"Great," said Willow sarcastically under her breath.

"Hey, Buff," Oz said, casually draping his arm over Willow's shoulder. She immediately shook it off.

"Don't do that," she growled.

"What?" said Oz. "What's wrong?"

"Nothing. I just don't like you touching me."

Oz and Buffy both stared at Willow.

"Since when?" asked Oz at last.

"Since whenever," said Willow. Her eyes had narrowed, her tone was cold. "Since I don't need anything from you, certainly not some kind of physical expression to show I belong to you!"

Oz stepped back, aghast. It was an expression Buffy didn't even believe he had in his repertoire, and it made him look like somebody else entirely. "What is the matter with you?" he demanded. "And where's the Three Stooges charm? You said you'd never take it off."

"Nothing's wrong," said Willow. "And I don't know where the bracelet and charm went—sorry." Then she smiled a normal Willow smile. "Hey, see you guys around!" And off she went down the hall, her auburn hair swinging beneath a bight blue knit cap.

"What's with her?" Oz asked Buffy.

Buffy watched her friend as she was swallowed up in the moving student bodies, and shook her head. "I'm not exactly sure," she said slowly. "But I have my suspicions. I'm not going to lose Willow to them. I'm going to find out what's happening if it kills me."

"Don't let it kill you, Buffy," said Oz. "We don't work without you."

"Yeah," Buffy said, her heart sinking with the thought that Willow had really changed into a Moon wannabe—and with a gut-deep uncertainty as to what that might mean. "I guess so."

Pheromones.

That was the key. It had to be.

Buffy planned on skipping her after-lunch class, going with Xander to the library, and doing some research. It would be hard without Willow's computer expertise, but they had to try.

Pheromones. She'd learned about them in biology. Insects could attract each other with them. They could influence the behaviors of others by the scents they released from their creepy little insect bodies. Could the Moon family be affecting the behavior of others with the perfume they were wearing? Anything, of course, was possible. This was the Hellmouth, after all.

Willow had bowed out from eating with Buffy and Xander. She had an invitation to sit at one of the Moon sisters' tables, along with the growing group of loud, "Womyn Power"-T-shirt-wearing girls and the handful of boys who sat around the edges of their table like zombie groupies, running for napkins, food, and drinks when the Womyn told them to. Buffy tried her best to chew and swallow her bagel and hummus, but her mind wasn't on eating. She stared at the gathering, trying to interpret their movements, their expressions, and the occasional snippets of conversation that drifted across the cafeteria floor in her direction.

But if the scene had been observed by anyone who was not suspicious, it would have seemed nothing more than a very enthusiastic group of—well, high-school girls. With wimpy, hanger-on boyfriends. And rather pathetically overstated T-shirts.

Mama Moon came into the cafeteria with the boys' basketball coach. The library supervisor was dressed as if she were going to a board meeting, with a navy power suit and her black hair coiled around her head. Her earrings were many shades less gaudy that those of her daughters. She was speaking intently with the coach, her arm linked through his. The coach didn't seem to mind. In fact, he seemed dazed and content.

"You know," Buffy said to Xander, "I haven't noticed a strong perfume problem with Mama Moon."

"Me, either," said Xander, his mouth full of fries.

"Maybe hers is more subtle," said Buffy. "She was able to influence Giles. Maybe she's after the teachers, too, for whatever reason. Maybe adults don't need the major whiff of perfume that teens do. An age-difference thing."

"Maybe," said Xander. "But I can't smell Calli and Polly, either. I've got a cold and my nose is stuffed up."

"Be glad," said Buffy.

Lunch ended. Xander and Buffy headed for the library. Just past the principal's office, Cordelia caught up with them. She looked freaked.

"Okay," she said, holding her hands out as if trying to stop whatever Buffy or Xander might say first. "Do you have eyes? Do they work? Have you seen what the demons are up to? In addition to lots of other lowlifes, they've taken Willow Rosenberg under their wing! Willow is their good buddy now! Willow is going to be in the pageant! I mean, *Willow*, no offense!"

"You rarely offend us anymore," said Buffy.

"I thought they were going to sabotage the pageant,

and I was right. But you didn't want to listen to me, did you? Polly, Calli, and her mother have convinced Wayland Enterprises not to have a bathing-suit competition. They think it's degrading, now how messed up is that? That was my ticket to Hawaii!"

This was the opening Buffy needed. "We agree with you. Well, not so much about the bathing-suit thing . . ."

"I agree with you about the bathing-suit thing," interrupted Xander.

". . . but about the Moon sister stuff. Do you want to help do something about it? We're cutting class to research in the library."

Cordelia pulled herself together, tossed her head, and said, "Sure. I'm not good at looking up but I'm good at writing down!"

"Good enough," said Buffy.

The library was not locked, and the lights were on. They called for Giles. He didn't answer.

But Mo Moon did.

She came out of Giles's office, all smiles and graceful moves. "Hello, there!" she said. "Buffy. And your friends?"

"Xander and Cordelia," said Buffy, feeling as if by giving their names she was putting them in a vulnerable position. "We need Mr. Giles. He was going to help us look up something. On the computer. Where is he?"

"He's in the office involved in paperwork, I fear."

Buffy trotted over to the office and glanced in. Giles was there, staring at a supply catalog. He looked as if he was in a trance. "Giles?" Buffy called. He looked up, then looked back at the catalog. A chill went up Buffy's spine. She returned to her friends.

"I'd be happy to help," said Mo Moon. She stepped close to the three, and all three backed up. It probably looked way obvious to the woman, but Buffy couldn't do anything about it.

"No, that's all right," said Xander, looking around uneasily. "I'm sure you have other things to do. We're good with the computer." He glanced at Buffy. They were so *not* good with the computer. They'd always depended on Willow to get onto the Internet and find the information they needed.

"Not at all!" Mo Moon practically floated to the computer behind the counter, sat, and poised her fingers over the keyboard. Xander, Cordelia, and Buffy exchanged nervous glances. "What are you researching, dear?"

Dear. Gag! Buffy said nothing. They needed to go on now, to the Sunnydale public library, where there would be no Moons spying on them, and see if . . .

"Insects," said Xander. "That smelly stuff insects have. What did you call it, Buffy?"

Buffy glared at Xander.

But Mo filled in the blanks herself. "Pheromones? Doing a science-fair project on arthropods?"

"Sure," said Buffy. "Science fair. Bugs. With scents. Bugs that stink."

"Stinkbugs," said Cordelia.

Typing as quickly as Willow ever did, Mo Moon pulled up several sites and printed out a pile of articles on pheromones while Buffy and her friends shifted from foot to foot. Mo Moon handed the papers to Buffy with a grin. "Anything else?"

"No," said Buffy, stuffing the articles into her backpack. "This is just great. Thanks." With her teeth gritted, she went back into the hallway, Xander and Cordelia on her heels.

"That was worth as much as a three-dollar bill," said Buffy. "I needed to research manmade pheromones, perfume pheromones, unnatural you-can-now-control-others-with-a-mere-dousing-of-this-scent pheromones."

"Maybe there's something in the articles," said Xander.

But in her last-period class, Buffy pored over every word on every piece of paper, and there was nothing about perfume pheromones—except that most people believed perfumes attracted the opposite sex, which was proven wrong in clinical studies. The fabricated smell that proved to be the biggest turn-on for humans was cinnamon buns.

And the Moon sisters didn't smell like cinnamon buns.

On the way out of school, Buffy passed the student bulletin board only to find that the Moons' battle of the sexes was alive, well, and growing. There was a new petition stapled over that of Allison's demand to play boys' basketball.

It read:

"Men Against Womyn! Petition to Allow Males to Enter the Miss Sunnydale Pageant!"

And, of course, the signatures had already begun.

CHAPTER 7

Buffy dropped onto on a kitchen chair and put her head on the table.

"You okay, hon?" asked Joyce. She was peering into the refrigerator, deciding what to fix for dinner.

"Sure, fine," said Buffy. "Just tired."

Buffy was emotionally exhausted. It was worse than the physical exhaustion that came with battling vampires. She and Xander—Cordelia had had a pageant meeting after school—had spent two hours in Sunnydale's public library, researching pheromones with the help of an overly enthusiastic librarian. They'd come away with some articles on scents in the animal kingdom, both natural and manmade.

But none of it was any more helpful than what Mama Moon had printed out.

"Buffy? I could call out for pizza if that would perk you up. Would you like pizza?"

"Whatever is fine. And I'm okay."

Buffy ran her fingers through her hair and pulled tight. *Think,* she thought. *Think! Willow is under the Moons' influence, and Giles as well. Somehow, some way, I have to get them away from the influence until I can figure out what it is, where it comes from, and how to stop it.*

Tomorrow she planned on going to the library at Crestwood College, Sunnydale's contribution to higher education. They would surely have more information on file, or a couple of old professors of zoology and mythology who would love to share anything and everything they knew.

But what can I do now? Lock them up and throw away the key?

The phone rang. Buffy caught the receiver before her mother could get halfway across the floor.

"Hello?"

It was Willow, and she sounded furious. "And just what is wrong with you, Buffy? Would you mind telling me? I'm so embarrassed. Tell me what is the deal?"

Okay, thought Buffy. *Think before you speak.* "I've had a long day, sorry. I'm not sure what you're—"

"You are, too. You sure are! You're being a holdout!"

"Holdout?"

"You sit at your own table during lunch, you won't hang with us in the halls. You haven't signed the newest petition for Ashley, *or* the one about the bathroom mirrors, *or* the one to force the school board to hire a female custodian for our school. Men can't clean! Aren't you proud to be feminine, Buffy? I thought you, of all people, would wear the badge of femaleness proudly!"

"Whoa there," said Buffy, putting her hand to the receiver and lowering her voice. Maybe Willow was brainwashed, but Buffy wasn't going to let her say that. "Willow, I've never not been proud to be who I am. Let me amend that. I've gotten better about being proud of who I am. Just because I don't want to eat where the only thing I can smell is cheap perfume and the only conversational topic is how girls should pretty much rule everything, it doesn't mean I'm not a big bad female."

"Buffy?" Joyce had obviously heard the last part.

"Well," continued Willow, "we've been talking about you. This afternoon at The Laughing Greek. We think it's time you got with the program, wore our T-shirts, signed up for the Miss Sunnydale pageant, and chose a boys' team to protest until they let you try out."

"Willow, I wish you could hear yourself."

"I hear myself just fine. And tomorrow we expect you to eat lunch with us. Good-bye."

The line went dead. Buffy slowly put the receiver back, and Joyce leaned against the sink, watching with concern.

"Everything okay?" her mother asked.

"Okay is a relative term."

"Was that Willow?"

"Sort of." Buffy turned around and faced Joyce. Her mother knew she dealt with the supernatural, so she had some idea of the dangers her daughter faced, but she could have no idea of the immense variety of weird situations that could spring up in Sunnydale. "It's a boy-girl problem, believe it or not. The whole school is getting way messed up. There are fights every day now. Willow's part of it."

"It sounds bad," said Joyce.

"It is. There's a core group of girls who have decided to take over the school, to run it their way, and anybody who gets in their way—well, I don't think it'll be pretty. The leaders are two new girls named Polly and Calli Moon. It's like they want to be the princesses of the school, or the empresses, or goddesses, or something equally repulsive."

"What is Principal Snyder doing about it?"

"Nothing beyond a few announcements in the morning. Maybe he hopes it'll blow over."

"Maybe I should voice my concerns as a parent."

"I don't think it would do any good."

This wasn't the right thing to say. "No? Well, I may be a single parent and I may be busy with my job, but never let it be said I don't go out of my way when my daughter's well-being is concerned."

"I never said that."

"No, you didn't."

"Did Dad say that?"

"Not exactly."

"Mom, I shouldn't have said anything. Please don't worry about school. It'll be fine." Buffy tried a smile. She didn't want her mother involved with something that could be real trouble. "It'll blow over. Probably. I hope."

"Well, I don't know," said Joyce. Then she took a breath. "Speaking of your father, we need to make a decision on the mother-daughter fashion show or the hiking trip. It's less than two weeks away!"

Buffy felt her hands draw into fists. This was the last thing she needed to deal with. There were too many sides being taken these days. She didn't want to be part of it.

And so, though it was very unlike her to ignore her mother, she did. She changed the subject.

"Could I invite Willow to dinner tomorrow night?" she asked, forcing a smile. "I know you work late, but I can fix something simple. I want to mend bridges with Willow. Okay? I'll invite Giles, too. He's a good mediator."

Joyce saw the avoidance, but she slowly shook her head and let out a breath. "All right, Buffy. I'll say yes.

But pretty soon now you'll need to say yes to somebody, as well. Do you understand?"

Buffy nodded. "Sure. No prob." *And maybe,* she thought, *getting Giles and Willow together, alone, away from the Moons, I can talk and maybe knock—well, not knock—some sense into them.*

And if that doesn't work, I'll lock them up and throw away the key.

Xander caught up with Buffy at her locker the following morning after second period. Buffy had gone to two classes, to at least get credit for being present, but was now on her way to Crestwood College. Xander and Oz were also going to skip out of school and catch up with her in Oz's van, after they got some gas and put some air in the leaky tires. Buffy knew she could wait to ride with her friends, but she felt a need to walk and be alone.

"I'm sick and tired of the way Willow is acting," Xander said, looking furtively around like somebody who was getting ready to cut school. Which he was. "Did you see her today? Strutting like a freakin' she-wolf with a pack of . . . she-wolves. She wouldn't speak to Oz, and she talked to me like I was dirt. And she gave *you* a pretty cold shoulder."

"I know," Buffy said. "But she did accept my invitation to dinner tonight. And so did Giles. Okay, sure, I had to tell him this was a surprise dinner to welcome Mo Moon to Sunnydale, but he agreed. Maybe at my house, surrounded by nothing Moonish, I can talk to them. They *might* hear me."

Xander took a deep, pained breath.

"We're going to get to the bottom of this mess, Xander. By this afternoon, we may have enough information to do . . . something. Now, quit looking so guilty about leaving school."

"If we don't get to the bottom of it," Xander said, slamming Buffy's locker shut as she pulled out her last book, "we should round up the Moon girls and give them a serious cross-gendered mauling."

Yeah, thought Buffy.

Yeah, indeed, she thought again as she cut across the grass outside the front of the school and headed around the side. *And as soon as we know exactly what we're up against, we'll do what we have to do.*

The shortcut to Crestwood College took Buffy behind the school, across the football field, and beneath the bleachers to the street on the other side. She closed her eyes for a moment as she crossed the lime-striped field, savoring the warm sun and the gentle breeze.

If only this moment could last, she thought. *If only things could be normal for just a little . . .*

"*Buffy, help me . . . !*"

She stopped short and opened her eyes, every muscle clenched.

She didn't see anything at first, just the grassy field and the bleachers, which were now pretty close. There was no one around. Shadows from the trees that lined the fence by the field flickered like black fingers on the ground. The shadows beneath the bleachers were still and silent.

But there it was. A sparkle beneath the bleachers.

Movement.

Buffy sprinted silently to the bottom of the tall structure and bent down, crawling under it and listening, feeling. Her jaw was clenched painfully tight.

Then she saw them. Two figures beneath the far edge of the bleachers, where the shadows were darkest. And yet the strobing sparkle was a beacon to Buffy. It was the twinkle of expensive jewelry. Buffy bent down and silently wormed her way through the crisscrossing support beams.

Then she could see. Polly Moon was with a boy—Adam Shoemaker—a sophomore on the swim team. They were on the ground, and Polly was holding Adam by the throat, humming and scratching his neck with long, slow strokes. Dark gouges could be seen in spite of the shadows. The song was a pretty yet disturbing tune that made Buffy's gut twist.

Suddenly, Polly shoved Adam's face down into a rain puddle beside her, and held his face in the water as he thrashed weakly. His fingers clutched out from his sides, grabbing at blades of grass and chunks of mud, but he had no strength against this Womyn.

Were the Moon girls a mutant species of vampire, able to tolerate sunlight yet needing to kill in order to survive? Had they killed Brian Andrews and Ben Rothman the same way?

Buffy didn't give herself time to think any more. She charged Polly, ducking under beams and jumping others. Polly looked up, her eyes bright yet not surprised; the moment Buffy was within striking distance, the blond hopped up and skipped backward with quick and surprising agility, allowing Adam's head to fall with a *clunk-splash* back into the puddle.

Buffy took a flying kick at Polly, but the girl dodged her foot, giggling. Then Buffy delivered a powerful double strike with her fists, but Polly stooped and swayed, staying clear of the blows.

"Who *are* you?" Buffy demanded, but Polly only laughed.

Buffy turned to Adam and pushed the boy with her

foot, causing him to roll out of the puddle. His face was ashen.

"Look what you've done!" Buffy said.

"Oh, I know what I have done," said the girl. "And it's really no matter. What matters is the cause. You, Buffy Summers, would be such an asset if you'd let yourself."

"You know nothing about me."

"But I do. So does Calli. So does my mother. We are as sensitive to others' ... *differences* ... as you are. You've sensed something in us. And we've sensed something in you." Polly winked and stepped toward Buffy. Buffy stepped back, slipping one hand into her backpack and wrapping it around a wooden stake.

"You guys are warped," said Buffy. "Stirring up some unnecessary girl-power mess and then killing people, too!"

"Whatever," said Polly with a smirk. "But you need to know there will be nine positions of power in our new order. Allison and Willow are strong, but they won't rank above six or seven. You, though, would make a wonderful Number Three. With me as One and Calli as Two, of course. We told Willow she could be Three—but we lied."

Buffy had no idea what she meant, but she chided, "What if Calli wants to be Number One?"

Polly frowned and began twisting the strands of the double-loop opal necklace between her fingers. Buffy saw that she was also wearing Willow's birthstone bracelet. "She won't, because I'm the one who is doing most of the work. She won't dare!" Then she laughed suddenly and abruptly, and leaned forward, grabbing for Buffy's shoulders. Buffy whipped the stake from the backpack and jabbed it deep into Polly's chest.

Polly looked with wonder at the stake as it protruded

from her silky blouse. The bright opal necklace she wore snapped, and stones scattered. Buffy backed up, uncertain what was going to happen next. Adam made soft sputtering noises on the ground. At least he was still alive.

Then there was the sound of footsteps, and both girls turned to see the elongated shadows of two figures on the other side of the bleachers. Polly yanked the stake from her chest and tossed it at Buffy. Buffy watched with wonder as the wound in the girl's chest healed itself. Then Polly snatched up a handful of muddy opals and skipped off so quickly she appeared to shimmer into nothingness.

Buffy dropped to her knees in the mud and shook Adam to bring him around. But he was dead now, with something white and slimy running from his ears and down his neck.

Now voices could be heard, and they belonged to Principal Snyder and the field maintenance man. Buffy scrambled to her feet and dashed behind the nearest tree.

"I seen something happening back here," said the maintenance man. "Some fightin', something like that. With the trouble we've been havin' lately, I thought I should get you before I checked on it. Don't want no rabid students comin' after me for just doin' my job!"

"Yes, yes, whatever," said the principal. "I hope you didn't drag me out here for nothing. I'd just poured myself a cup of coffee."

From her hiding place Buffy wondered, *So he'd rather find trouble than be dragged out of his office for no reason? A fine example of maturity to the pupils of Sunnydale High much?*

Then the men found the body. The maintenance man

shrieked. Principal Snyder shook his head and rubbed his chin, looking more annoyed than sorry or shocked.

There is no way I can tell them the truth, Buffy thought as she watched the two men hurry off for help. *They might think I'm involved. I know Snyder wouldn't believe me—no matter what the truth is.*

Besides, she thought as she climbed over the fence on the other side of the tree and landed in a tall clump of buggy weeds, *I don't even know the whole truth yet!*

CHAPTER 8

Buffy hurried along the street, watching carefully to her left and right. The horn-honk behind her nearly made her jump out of her skin.

It was Oz's van. It slowed down beside her and Oz rolled down the driver's side window. "Hey!" he called. "I know you wanted to walk to the college, but I think you need to see something right away."

"And I need to tell you something right away," she said as she climbed into the passenger's seat. Xander was in the back, hunched over, quiet.

"What's with him?" she asked Oz.

"That's what you needed to see," said Oz. "We were getting ready to leave school. One of the Moon girls came over to Xander with her buddies in tow."

"It was Calli. Polly and I were already indisposed. I have to fill you in."

"Yeah," said Oz. "First, Xander. He had told me he was immune to whatever pheromones they were putting off 'cause of some cold blocking his ability to smell. So he told Calli he thought the Womyn were festering boils on the noble face of feminism. Something Xanderish like that. They didn't care. Calli just grabbed him and laughed in his face like it was the funniest thing she ever heard. Now—"

"Now," said Xander listlessly. "Now, now, now."

". . . He's just like those Zomb-Boys who hang with the Moons," said Oz. He took a deep, angry breath. "He's totally out of it."

Buffy grabbed Xander's hand over the back of her seat. "Xander, what happened? Can you tell me?"

Xander's eyes went in and out of focus. "Hey, Buff," he said. "Aren't those Moon girls bomb?"

"Damn," said Buffy, sitting back hard in her seat. She felt sick—sick for Xander, sick for Willow, sick for Giles, and sick for the dead boys. "Oz, I caught Polly doing something to Adam Shoemaker behind the football bleachers. Well, something is a bit of an understatement. She killed him. Sang to him, scratched his neck, stuck his face in a puddle, did something to mess up his head. When I tried to stake her, there was no blood, no screaming, no writhing in pain or anything! Major disappointment. Now I'm thinking these girls—or whatever they are—are not only taking over the minds of kids at school, but they may have killed Brian Andrews and Ben Rothman, too."

Oz had turned a corner and was heading for the college, but Buffy stopped him. He pulled to the curb.

"I've got to rethink all this," she said, rubbing her forehead. "It's not pheromones clearly, because Xander couldn't smell Calli and she still got to him. It's something else. Drop me off at the police department. I'm going to ask what the autopsies revealed on the two boys who drowned. You take Xander home. Hey, Xander."

Xander glanced up slowly. It was heartbreaking to see him like this.

"You have to do what I say, understand?" Buffy said.

Xander nodded dully. "Men must do what women tell them."

"Listen to him!" hissed Oz. "Disgusting!"

"It sure is," said Buffy. "Xander, Oz is going to take you home. I don't want you to come to school any more until things are safe. Until I tell you to, okay?"

"I should stay home?" asked Xander.

"Until I tell you it's safe."

Xander shrugged. "Okay, Buffy."

And as Oz sped toward the police station, Buffy reached back and held Xander's hand. She wished she had all the answers. She was supposed to have them, but she didn't, and it was unfair—so unfair—that so much bad happened and she couldn't always stop it.

Even though she was the Slayer, and she was supposed to.

"Now, you stupid, hardheaded demon, will you believe me at last?" snarled Viva.

On the floor of the old Beanie Baby shop, the vampire Nadine was writhing in exquisite pain, bubbles of foam pooling from the corners of her mouth and smearing her hawk-sharp nose. Her lips were curled back from her fangs, and the sound emanating from her throat was a sound Viva had heard before. It was the sound of a vampire dying from poisoned blood.

Becky and Barb stood by, watching in horrified amazement. Other female vampires, many of whom had trusted that Nadine was right and Viva was wrong, leaned against the wet basement wall and glared furiously at their dying friend as if she was doing all this on purpose.

Nadine's tongue was swollen and blistered, and when

she spoke it was barely coherent. "One of those geeky boys who hang outside the Greek restaurant waiting for their girlfriends," she managed. "Such an easy target he was. I just waited until none of the other boys were looking, wiggled my finger at him from around the alley corner, and he came over. Like he trusted me or something. Ohhhhh!" She grimaced, rolled to her side, and drew up her knees. Lesions had formed on her neck and hands, and were oozing clear liquid. Viva knew this would happen. She'd tried to warn Nadine, but Nadine never listened.

"He tasted fine," Nadine garbled, gasping for breath, "but once I got back here, it started. Owww!"

Viva pointed at the dying vampire and spoke to the others. "I told you this would happen! Now you all have to believe me! More of you have to help me catch that Slayer! More vampires are going to die this way if we don't get her to work for us!"

But to Viva's surprise, the others—including Barb and Becky—shook their deformed heads. "We'll get the Moons," said Barb. "But Viva, just freakin' forget the Slayer! We tried that, it didn't work. Let's handle one major disaster at a time. We find the Slayer, kill her, no problem. But this Moon business is something we have to do ourselves."

"We'll watch their place every night," said Becky. "Jump their skinny, pretty little butts and tear them a couple new breathing holes!"

"Yeah!" said Barb.

"Yeah!" chorused some of the other vampires.

"It won't kill them," protested Viva. "They don't *die* like that! But the Slayer—"

"Enough," said Becky. She got in Viva's face, her never-pigmented skin even more translucent than ever, the once-living veins showing a stark greenish blue beneath it. "We don't need the cursed Slayer for anything! Get it? We are all-powerful! We'll take care of it ourselves!"

Viva snarled.

"Get it?"

"No!" retorted Viva. "But *you'll* get it—and you'll die from it!"

"I'm smarter than Nadine," said Becky. "I'll know."

On the floor, Nadine screamed, gurgled, and died.

The police station was a bust. Buffy had gone there, trying hard to look nondescript and harmless, explaining she was with the Sunnydale High School student newspaper and was writing a report on the terrible events of the past weeks. Like the deaths of Brian Andrews, Ben Rothman, and now, Adam Shoemaker. But she'd gotten no farther than Policewoman Kincaid at the front desk. No matter how Buffy explained that she didn't want to know about suspects or leads in the case, that all she wanted to know was what was in the autopsy reports, Policewoman Kincaid wouldn't budge. She just stared at Buffy as if Buffy were a minor irritant in a long day of irritations.

Okay, Buffy thought as she left the place. *I'm not one to give up. I'll find out what I need to know one way or the other.*

She went to the funeral home by way of the Sunnydale Cemetery—in which she had had, oh, more than a few pulse-racing, vampire- 'n' fun-filled adventures. It was almost one-thirty, and the funeral home often kept bankers' hours, closing at two unless there was an actual service scheduled. She had to see for herself. If no one would let her see an official report, she would make an official report of her own.

Sunnydale Funeral Home was an historic building, through which many of the town's well-known and little-known deceased had passed on their way to a six-foot-deep plot in Sunnydale Cemetery or a vase on a living room mantle. The funeral home's motto, emblazoned on the sign in the front, was "We'll take care of the rest."

From across the street, Buffy watched the funeral home, which stood next to the locked-tight Dilly-Dally Daycare Center. Swings in the playground swayed back and forth in the afternoon breeze, squeaking forlornly; small animals skittered about the seesaws and slides, scouring for snack crumbs the children might have left behind. *Good luck,* Buffy thought. *This place was shut down two months ago after a child broke his arm on the swing set. If there are any crumbs left, they'll be petrified by now.*

At two o'clock, a car drove out from the rear parking lot and onto the road. Another left at two-fifteen. By two-forty-five Buffy was certain there was no one left in the funeral home, at least no one who could do anything about her sneaking inside. She ran across the street and around the side, to a window over a thick row of box-woods. It didn't take much pounding with one of the sharp stakes to crack the glass; then she wrapped her hand in the sleeve of her jacket and slammed it the rest of the way through. With a flick of the side latches and a lifting of the pane and screen, she was able to slide inside. No alarms went off. A surprise—and a relief.

I've got a couple of bucks in my account, she thought as she stood on top of the glass shards in what was probably a family receiving room. *I'll mail it to the funeral home anonymously to help with the repairs.*

Both Ben and Brian were still here, awaiting burial. It was going to be a "Sunnydale High Says Good-Bye To

Two of Its Own" deal, the day after tomorrow at the cemetery. A kind of deal Sunnydale High had a lot of right now, unfortunately. Adam was probably still at the medical examiner's. This was the easier pick of the two places, and there were clues to be found. She knew it. And she hoped she was sensitive enough to pick up on them and use them to help her friends, her school, and her town. Without Willow, Xander, or Giles.

In a small viewing room were two closed coffins, surrounded by baskets of flowers and covered with massive, colorful sprays. Buffy checked to make sure the blinds were drawn tightly over the window, then clicked on a small table lamp. She gazed at the caskets. One was a shiny mahogany, the other a burnished ebony. Both the same style caskets with identical brass handles and trim. Ben and Brian's mothers were friends. Maybe they had chosen the coffins together. Buffy could imagine them, side by side, weeping as they tried to decide which boxes were the most appropriate, tasteful, comfortable. So sad.

Think about that later, Buffy, or you'll never get this done, she thought.

She went to the mahogany casket and put her hands on the polished wood, thinking a good thought for whoever was inside. Then immediately she wiped the area off with the edge of her jacket. She would not leave any traces of her presence here. With her hands drawn up inside the sleeves, she slowly lifted the cover of the casket.

Inside was Ben Rothman. His dark hair had been combed and sprayed. His once-handsome face was tinted just enough so that he looked, well, more alive than an average vampire or ghoul. That was good, she guessed.

She examined the scratches on his neck. They'd been

made up, but she spat on her fingers and wiped as much of the makeup away as she could. The marks were identical to those she'd seen Polly make on Adam Shoemaker. She gritted her teeth against distaste and stuck her pinky deep in his ear. It came out with a dry white substance that was not any kind of earwax she'd ever come across—not that she'd done much earwax collecting in her time. But Adam's ears had been draining something white and sticky. This, she was sure, was the same stuff.

She closed the coffin lid and went to the second one. She opened it to find Brian Andrews, made up much like Ben except someone had thought it would be nice to give him an "eternal-rest smile." It looked more like he had bitten into an electrical wire. She felt his neck—same scratches. She scraped the same dry white substance from inside his ear. She tore a sheet of notepaper from a pad on the reception desk and folded the dry crumbs into a neat little packet. This stuff, she knew, was very important. She put the folded paper packet into her pocket.

One of Brian's eyelids was slightly open. Buffy pulled the lid up all the way, then the other. "What did you see? What did you hear?" she asked the body uneasily. "Have you been calling me? Trying to tell me that the Moon sisters murdered you?"

Just then the overhead light blared on, and Buffy jumped. She spun about to face Joe Bruce, the young assistant funeral-director-in-training, in his director-in-training bow tie and brown jacket. His eyes were huge, his mouth dropped open. "W-what is going on?" he demanded.

"Mr. Bruce!" Buffy shouted, her heart thundering. "I'm sorry, I didn't mean to startle anybody!"

Mr. Bruce stared at her for a moment. He looked more scared than angry. "Who are you?"

"I . . . um," began Buffy. This was not wonderful. What to say? "I, uh—I'm Brian's girlfriend. I had to see him. Alone. Without his family around. They are such busybodies. Nosey. You know the type." She sniffed for effect.

"You broke in." It was more a question than a statement.

"I guess you could say that. It was grief that made me. Please understand. I had to see Brian again. Alone."

A face passed Joe's shoulder. It was a girl in her late teens, disheveled hair, wary. "Joe? What's she doing here? What's happening?"

Buffy knew what was happening, at least with deer-in-the-headlights Joe Bruce. He'd been having a little rendezvous with Miss Bad Hair Day somewhere in the privacy of this quiet, dark little place of business. *Yuck!*

"It's okay," said Mr. Bruce, clearing his throat. "I'm just sending her out."

"Mr. Bruce," said Buffy carefully. "Could I have five more minutes with Brian? Please?" She forced her lower lip to tremble. "Then I promise I'll leave."

"No, you have to go now."

Buffy grabbed Brian's body and pulled it halfway out of the coffin. She began to sob in big whoops, clutching the dead boy. "Oh, please, please, let me be with him just a bit longer! I miss him terribly and will never see him again! Please, Mr. Bruce, please?"

"Joe, that's pretty damn sad," said the young woman. "Give her a few minutes."

"Please?" wailed Buffy. The body was heavy, and she had to dig her fingers in the shoulders to keep from dropping it. The dead eyes watched her steadily. "And you don't have to tell anybody I was here. Okay?" Buffy gazed at Mr. Bruce to give him the very clear message: *I won't tell on you if you don't tell on me. Deal?* "Okay, Mr. Bruce?"

It was a deal. "Okay, I guess," said Mr. Bruce. He straightened and tried to look professional. "Five minutes. Then let yourself out the front. I'll lock the door behind you." He clicked off the overhead light.

Buffy listened to their footsteps retreating on the carpet runner. Then she looked at Brian. "What did the Moons do to you?" she asked him. "Did you really drown, or was it something else?"

What she saw next made her nearly drop the body onto the floor. Through the dead, open eyes, Buffy could see faint light. She turned the body so it was directly in front of the lamp on the small table. It seemed unbelievable, but it was true. Light from the lamp was visible through the lifeless orbs of Brian Andrews's eyes, like light glowing through a nightmarish jack-o'-lantern. The lamplight was shining through Brian's head and out his eyes.

Because there was nothing to block the light but a little bone and skin.

Brian Andrews had no brain.

It was gray matter that had poured from his ear. The dried crusts in the folded paper in Buffy's pocket was dried brain. Polly Moon hadn't drowned these boys. She'd wanted it to look that way, but that wasn't what had happened. She had been much more creative, much more evil.

Oh, my God, Buffy thought, her throat dry. *She liquefied their minds!*

CHAPTER 9

Buffy had exactly half an hour to fix dinner, by the time she'd gotten home, changed out of her digging-for-brain-matter wear, taken a hot shower, and called Oz with the disturbing update. Oz said he would come and help her with the dinner, and that he'd be there in twenty minutes. It was five-thirty. Willow and Giles were due to arrive at six.

With hair not completely blow-dried, Buffy hastily set the table with three plates and settings of flatware, folded some paper towels under the forks, and lit a candle for the center of the table.

But then she stopped in her tracks. She had no idea what she would actually cook. Not that there was royalty coming to dine, but the meal had to be decent enough for them to stay. And actually eat. And hear her out.

"Maybe I should have hired Mr. Gianakous to make something," she said humorlessly as she pawed through the fridge and the cabinets.

Then she found a boxed taco dinner behind the saltine crackers. *Yes! I can do tacos!*

In the fridge was half a head of lettuce, two tomatoes,

and a block of not-completely-moldy cheddar. There was no ground beef, though. *Vegetarian tacos, that's okay, that's cool, that's today.* She shaved the mold off the cheese, whacked the block into uneven chunks, diced the tomatoes and chopped the lettuce. The taco shells went into the oven to warm.

Hurry up hurry up! Calm down calm down!

At 5:52 the doorbell rang. *Oz, yes, good timing!* Buffy thought. Everything was ready, except her hair had gone weird in the rush. She ran her brush through it, threw the brush on the sofa, glanced in the living-room mirror, then reached for the front doorknob and pulled the door open.

Willow, Calli, and Polly stood on the front porch, smiling and holding plates of food. Willow was in the center of the three, with Polly and Calli each holding on to her arms as if they were Dorothy, the Scarecrow, and the Tin Man all ready to skip off to Oz. The place, that is.

"Hi, Buffy!" said Willow. "I invited Calli and Polly along since they wanted to see where you lived and, well, they really want to get to know you better. I knew you wouldn't mind if we brought extra food. See?" She nodded at her tray. "Biscuits!"

"You're early," said Buffy, staring at Polly, who stared back with a smiling, *Oh, but don't we know each other a little bit better since this afternoon?* look on her face.

"Just a few minutes. Better early than late, right? Calli brought chips and dip, although you might already have that, sorry if you do. Polly made . . ."

Buffy wasn't listening to what Polly Moon had brought. She was envisioning herself attacking the sisters, punching them and throwing them from the porch, then grabbing Willow. She could see the plate of chips and dip arching in the air and hitting the porch like a Scud missile, and the biscuits falling in a doughy hail.

But she blinked, clearing her head. Because she knew she couldn't do that.

Not now.

She had seen Polly's speed, incredible strength, and imperviousness to dying by the stake. She had seen Adam Shoemaker's dead body lying on the ground behind the bleachers, his brain drained away. Yes, Willow was a girl, and so far these blond beauties had killed no females. But just as clearly as Buffy could imagine herself striking the sisters with every ounce of her strength, she could imagine those slim, bejeweled fingers ripping Willow's arms from the sockets as the blows came. She could imagine their tinkling, spiteful laughter as Willow lay dying.

No. Not like this. I need a better plan.

"Um . . . ," said Buffy, coughing into her hand and shivering. "I'm sick. Can't have dinner tonight. Sorry. I must have caught something this afternoon."

"Oh?" Willow sounded truly disappointed.

"Yeah, can't let you in. Bummer. So. I'll see you guys later, then?"

"Well, all right," Willow said with a frown. "The dip was avocado, too."

Buffy looked at Polly. Polly grinned at Buffy. *This is a temporary standoff,* Buffy thought. *So wipe that smirky smile right off your face, devil girl. You're gonna go down soon, and bigger than you can imagine.*

Buffy closed the door and went back to the living-room window to watch the three retreating into the night.

"Willow," Buffy said aloud. "I'll get you out of this. I will! Nothing will stop me." She turned from the window.

There was another knock on the door. *Willow? You came back. You saw my face and somewhere deep inside you knew the danger!*

Buffy opened the door.

Oz stumbled inside, slamming the door behind him. "Don't like to stay outside alone very long. Something to do with vampires, you might have heard."

"Yeah, I've heard."

"Sorry I'm late. Tire went flat again, had to get air."

"Did you see Willow leaving?" Buffy asked.

"No." Oz looked concerned. "Was she here already?"

"Yep. With the Barbie twins. I couldn't let them in, of course. I have to think of some other way to get Willow out of this."

"And Giles . . . ?"

There was thumping on the porch, then the door. Oz yanked it open.

Giles stood there, looking confused, holding a wind-blown bunch of daisies in one hand. "Buffy?" he said, his eyes squinting from behind his glasses. "Did you invite me to dinner tonight? I think you did. Am I correct?"

"Giles! Yes!" Buffy grabbed his elbow and pulled him through the door. She slammed it shut and took the flowers.

"Those are for Ms. Moon," said Giles. "Has she arrived yet? You did say this was a surprise dinner for her?"

"Yes I did and no she's not," said Buffy. "I'll put the flowers in a jar for now. You . . . you can give them to Ms. Moon later. Why don't we all go in the kitchen. Hear me?"

Giles looked at Oz, then said, "I've parked several houses down the street. I couldn't quite remember which was your house."

"Come on, Giles," said Oz.

The Watcher followed them into the kitchen, and sat at the table. He stared into the candle. Tiny, twin flames danced on the lenses of his glasses.

Oz and Buffy sat across from Giles. Buffy took Giles's hand in hers and said, "You've taught me a lot over the past few years. I've listened to you—well, *most* of the time I've listened to you. Now you have to listen to me."

"Where is Mo?"

"Mo isn't coming," said Oz.

"Giles," said Buffy. "There is some sort of magic going on, some kind of bad mojo that I haven't figured out. And I will. But hear me. You are not yourself. You have been affected by Mo Moon somehow, and you are doing what she tells you to do even though it's wrong."

Giles blinked and looked away from the candle. Maybe Buffy had hit a nerve.

She went on. "She's evil, Giles. She and her daughters. They're responsible for not just the bad boy-girl stuff happening at school, but the deaths of Ben, Brian, and Adam. They're killers, Giles. And we have to stop them. Do you understand me?"

Giles said nothing for a long moment. *It's getting through!* Buffy thought. She looked hopefully at Oz, who just shrugged.

But then the man stood up. "If Mo's not coming, I'm going home."

Buffy jumped up, knocking her chair over, and blocked the kitchen door. "Wait! We're talking fate of the city here, maybe much more! You're the Watcher, I'm the Slayer. We are here at the Hellmouth to stop supernatural evil from overrunning the world. Remember? It's what we *do!* Stopping the bad guys! Snap out of it!"

Giles looked at Buffy, then Oz. He said slowly, "I'm going home. Mo's not here. You lied to me."

"No, you can't go. You're a male! You're in mortal danger!"

"Get out of my way," said Giles. "Let me leave."

"Oz!" shouted Buffy. "Get the basement door!"

"Huh—?" began Oz.

But Buffy grabbed Giles's arms behind his back and said, "Now! It's the only way!"

Oz sprinted to the door and yanked it open. With Giles struggling and twisting, harder than Buffy would have imagined for his foggy and forgetful manner, she forced him forward and down the rough, wooden stairs.

"Need any help?" Oz called from upstairs.

"Get down here!" Buffy shouted, and a second later Giles locked his legs and the two of them fell the remaining four steps, hitting the hard flooring with a thud.

"Ohhh," said Buffy. She'd landed on her shoulder, with Giles's legs across her.

"Let me go home," said Giles, his face pressed to the floor, his voice muffled.

Oz hit the bottom step. He looked baffled. "Are we going to tie him up?"

"You have a better idea?" asked Buffy. "If not, then this is the only solution for now, as bad as it seems." She pushed Giles off her and stood up shakily. Giles still lay on the floor, blinking, his breath stirring tiny dust bunnies to life. Buffy took his arms and Oz his legs and, lifting him as best they could, they hauled him to the far side of the cellar where some old sleeping bags lay in a heap.

"I'm so sorry," Buffy said as she and Oz bound the man's hands and feet with a towel Buffy had ripped apart. "You don't know how sorry, and I hope you won't remember much of this. But it won't be for long, I promise. A day or two. Three, tops. I'll bring water and food and stuff. We don't have rats or mice or anything. Well." She and Oz stood up straight, dusted off their hands, and looked at the befuddled, bound man in the corner. "Sleep well, okay?"

Giles eyes rolled away from her, and he looked at the damp basement walls.

"He meant to say okay," said Oz. "But the gag. You know."

The Moon sisters were enthralled by sparkly jewelry, that was very clear. It seemed very *not* what they were all about in regard to Womyn Power, yet there it was. Every day they wore new strands and rings of precious gemstones, obtained, it seemed, by merely telling their followers that they wanted what wasn't theirs and getting it handed over to them without question or pause.

Buffy and Oz caught Cordelia between first and second period just outside the school's main office. Down the hall near the restrooms, an argument was brewing between a crowd of girls and a crowd of boys. It had to do with the number of toilets in the respective restrooms, what was fair and what wasn't, blah, blah, blah. The voices were loud and furious. Principal Snyder's morning reminders weren't cutting much mustard.

"I broke into the funeral home last evening and you can't imagine what I discovered," Buffy said to Cordelia.

"Probably dead people?"

Buffy went on. "Yes, sure. Now listen carefully. The Moon sisters killed Brian, Ben, and Adam. But the guys weren't drowned. They got their brains melted. Came out their ears. Pretty gross."

Cordelia frowned. "Melted their brains? Okay, back up some. Play fill-in-the-blanks."

"I looked in the coffins. I picked up Brian and could see light through his eyes, shining in from behind."

"Disgusting!" said Cordy.

"But why would they kill anybody when they seem to be able to control people so easily?" asked Cordy.

Buffy shrugged.

"Okay, how do we stop them?"

"I don't know yet," said Buffy. "But I want to test something first. Something that is just weird enough to be important. Maybe."

"Maybe," said Oz.

"Or maybe not," said Buffy. "Give me your ankle bracelet."

"What?" squeaked Cordy. "Absolutely not!"

"Those little stones aren't real diamonds, are they?"

Cordy sputtered, looking royally offended. Then she said in a very low, angry voice, "Rub it in that my father lost most of his money for not paying taxes, why don't you?"

"But are they real? Can you spare them to save Sunnydale High?"

Exasperated, Cordy said, "Okay, so they're diamonaires, but they look like the real thing. Modern technology has gone a long way toward improving the laboratory-created gemstone. I'm not ashamed! And if you tell anybody, I'll kill you."

"I won't need to say a thing," said Buffy.

Cordy went into the bathroom to take off the bracelet. She came back out and pressed it into Buffy's hand. "This better be good," she said coolly.

Each day after lunch, the growing Moon entourage tended to take the same parade route around the school before breaking off to their various classrooms. Out the front door, around the fountain in the courtyard to pause and do a little proselytizing from the brick walkway to whoever was hanging around, then back inside, down the library hall, and back up past the gym and restrooms, stopping at last in an artery-clogging cluster by the student lounge to watch for new recruits.

Oz, Cordelia, and Buffy walked a good ten yards ahead of the wave of Womyn and their men today, kind of like the banner holders before the band in the parade, but without the banner. *Or the marching boots. Or the smiles,* Buffy thought. They pretended to be chatting while dropping an occasional diamonaire from Cordelia's disassembled ankle bracelet in the path of the oncoming wave. Buffy glanced over her shoulder every few moments to watch the progression of her experiment.

And the results were what she expected. Neither Polly nor Calli Moon seemed capable of passing by the sparkling pseudo-gem on the floor without bending to snatch it up and put it in her pocket. They were quick, they were smooth, stooping and collecting without breaking stride. Nobody else in their group of friends noticed what was happening.

But the Moon sisters did.

As Buffy and Oz passed the student bulletin board, Buffy thumbtacked the ankle bracelet with its remaining two stones to the cork. Not ten seconds later, Calli spied it as she went past and, with the speed of a cobra, grabbed it off, slipped it onto her wrist, and went back to talking to Willow and Allison about a song she was writing for the opening number of the Miss Sunnydale Pageant.

Buffy pulled Oz and Cordelia into a locker alcove. The Moon group ambled by.

"I was right," said Buffy. "The test group—Polly and Calli—took the bait. The control group—all the Moon groupies—couldn't have cared less. You know what this means, don't you?"

Oz raised one brow. "No, what?"

Buffy's shoulders fell. "I don't know, either. I was hoping you'd figured it out. Thought maybe it would ring some kind of bell in your head."

"Not even a gong."

"You mean I gave up my bracelet for nothing?" asked Cordelia.

"Not nothing," said Buffy. "Be patient. Okay. Anyway. The Moons are way too dangerous to have on our campus. We know that much. They've done a lot of damage, some of which I hope is reparable. We've got to figure this out. We're *going* to figure this out." She forced her voice to sound strong, but her jaw shook. *Willow. Xander. Giles. Who's next?* She couldn't think of it. She couldn't afford to get scared, at least no more than she already was.

Oz touched her shoulder. "I'm with you, Nancy Drew. I want Willow back." His eyes looked suddenly tight, and Buffy knew he was fighting his own battle with worry. As soon as they knew what they were dealing with, they would do the cross-gendered butt kicking Xander had recommended. Before he'd changed. *Poor Xander!*

The bell sounded.

"Meet me after school," said Buffy.

"Will do," said Oz.

"Pageant practice," said Cordy with a shrug.

Buffy took off down the hall toward her classroom, knowing that on top of melted brains and dead students, the last thing she needed was another tardy slip.

After the last bell of the day sounded, Buffy made a quick pit stop at her locker, then pushed her way toward the front door. She had paid no attention in her last classes, but had sat with pen and notebook scribbling down anything she could think of that was odd about the Moon family. The perfume. The jewelry. The attitude. The grabbing and laughing. The brain-melting talent. The resistance to being killed by sharp, stabbing things.

Together, these held the answer to the brainwashing and murders. Willow would have been the best one to help Buffy piece together the truth. But Willow was indisposed. As were Xander and Giles. And, well, Cordelia. But Buffy had Oz. The two of them would find the key to stopping this cancer.

Then she saw her mother in the hallway, talking to a smiling, laughing Mo Moon.

Joyce Summers had left work at the art gallery early that afternoon. What Buffy had told her about the division growing in the school had played on her mind, reminding her of the racial tensions in her own high school years ago. Sunnydale wasn't supposed to be that kind of place. Joyce was going to make sure the staff of the high school knew how she felt, and that she wouldn't sit still for it.

Principal Snyder was in his office, his hands in his pockets, staring out the window at a spot of sunlight on the campus lawn. After passing muster with the secretary, Joyce knocked on the principal's door, then went in after several long moments passed with no answer.

"Mr. Snyder?" she asked.

The man didn't move for a full fifteen seconds, and Joyce felt odd, as if she'd come in on some very private moment. But then he looked over his shoulder. "Yes?"

"Mr. Snyder," she said, standing in front of his desk, picking her words carefully. She'd never liked this little man. "I'm Joyce Summers. Buffy Summers's mother? I wanted to drop in for a moment to share a concern. I know you are doing a fine job here at the high school. I can't imagine having to be responsible for so many young people."

"Mmm," said the principal, turning toward her, his head tilting. It seemed his mind was on something else entirely.

"But Buffy mentioned a problem brewing here," Joyce continued, "and I felt it necessary to let you know that I am disturbed by what I've heard. A band of girls trying to take over the school, causing tensions and conflicts."

"Conflicts?" The man's brows drew together. "We don't have any conflicts."

"Girls insisting that everything be the way they want it. Putting down boys for, well, being born boys. Could you tell me what you are planning on doing about it before it gets any worse?"

The principal put his palms flat on his desk and stared at a stack of papers by his phone. He puffed his cheeks in and out with air. Then he looked up again. "Hello, there. What can I do for you?"

"Mr. Snyder?" said Joyce. What was wrong with this man? It was as if he'd forgotten she was even there. "I was asking you about the problem with the girls."

"The girls? There is nothing wrong with our girls. Our Sunnydale High girls are our pride."

"The boy-girl arguments, they're getting out of hand—"

"Nothing is out of hand, Mrs . . . ?"

"Ms. Summers," said Joyce. "I'd heard that—"

"Nothing is out of hand, Ms. Summers," said Principal Snyder. "Good afternoon, and thank you for stopping by."

He turned back to the window and stared out at the sun.

Joyce watched him for a moment, then left the office.

She would write to the parent-teacher association and the school board. She would write the mayor if necessary. If the principal wanted to play an "I know nothing" game, so be it. Joyce could play hardball. Buffy deserved as much. The other students here deserved as much.

"Ms. Summers?"

Joyce turned to see a woman she'd never met before, with a finely tailored suit and black hair pinned neatly to her head, coming toward her amid the swarming students with her hand outstretched. She was a very pretty woman.

"Ms. Summers?" she said cheerfully. "Hello, it's so nice to meet you. I'm Mo Moon, acting library supervisor."

"Hello," said Joyce. She took the other woman's hand. The grip was just a little too firm, and Joyce had to wrangle her hand back. "Do you know me?"

"I know your daughter, Buffy," said Mo. "A delightful girl! I just wanted to introduce myself and ask if you'd gotten one of the fliers for the Women's Society? I would love to have you come to our first meeting. I'm not certain of the date yet until I get out and about the community more and gauge the schedules of the ladies. I've been busy with chores here at the school, but that will ease up very soon. May I put you on the list as a yes?"

"Oh, well, I'll have to see," said Joyce. "Did you say your last name was Moon? Do you have two girls who are new to Sunnydale High?"

"Yes!" said Ms. Moon. "Calli and Polly. I couldn't be prouder of them. They seem to be adjusting well. Making lots of friends."

Joyce remembered the names Polly and Calli as the girls responsible for the trouble. "Mo, what do you know about the boy-girl problem here at the school?"

Mo laughed and reached for Joyce's shoulders. Joyce took a step backward. She didn't like this immediate assumption that she was Mo's good friend. "Oh, troubles between boys and girls will always be there," said Mo. "We had troubles when we were younger. These kids will have troubles, too. Don't you remember your school days, all the bickering?"

"Well, some, I suppose . . ."

"I have nine daughters," said Mo with a smile. "Can you believe it? Only two are with me now, but yes, I've been blessed! I know at this age girls can be emotional and dramatic. I bet Buffy gets that way at times. I don't worry much about it. My girls are just trying to find their way here. It's hard being new."

"Nine daughters?" said Joyce. Good Lord, she couldn't imagine what that would be like.

"Yes," said Mo. "Listen, why don't we go out for a cup of coffee? The day is over, and we could talk. I'd enjoy that. Would you like to?"

"Well . . . ," said Joyce. It would be a nice gesture to help welcome this new woman to town. Maybe she was right about her daughters just trying to assert themselves in a new environment. Maybe Buffy was overreacting a little. "All right. For a little while."

"Good!" said Ms. Moon. And again, she reached out for Joyce's shoulders and this time Joyce, trying to be understanding and friendly, did not back away.

At that very moment, Buffy slammed into her mother from the side, knocking her out of her shoes and onto the floor.

"Buffy!" cried Joyce. "What did you do that for?"

Buffy held out her hand to her mother. She could feel Mo Moon's burning stare on her back. So be it. The woman could fume all she wanted. She wasn't going to get her supernatural claws on Joyce Summers.

"Sorry, Mom," said Buffy as Joyce stood and brushed off her backside and hands. "I saw you and was running to give you a hug. I slipped."

Joyce gave Buffy an *oh-give-me-a-break* look. Buffy knew she didn't believe her but that didn't matter. Not now. Now she had to get Joyce out of here. She slipped her arm through her mother's and walked her to the door.

"Just what was that?" Joyce insisted once they were out on the sidewalk. "I don't think I broke anything, but you never know! Tailbones are fragile."

"I'm sorry," said Buffy sincerely. "It was an accident."

"It didn't feel much like an accident."

Buffy wanted to go no farther down this path. "What were you doing here?"

"I came to see the principal about the troubles you were telling me about. The boy-girl thing."

"Yeah? What did he say?"

"Not much. He was acting very strangely. Preoccupied. Hazy. Forgetful."

I wonder if Mo Moon has gotten to him like she has Giles and the football coach? Buffy wondered.

"So . . . I thought I'd go to the school board."

Uh-oh! "Mom," said Buffy. "I honestly wish I hadn't said anything. You're making it a major when it's so minor."

"Buffy," said Joyce. She really sounded put out, hurt even. "I'm trying my best to be a good mother."

"And you are, really. Maybe I was just overreacting. They're . . . just irritating and I let it get to me."

"That's what Ms. Moon said."

"She did?"

"Yes." Joyce looked over toward her car, hesitating, as

if there was more she wanted to say or more she needed to hear before she left.

"Mom," said Buffy. "Thanks for checking on things. You're great. I know I don't say that very often."

That was it. Joyce smiled and gave Buffy a hug. "Thanks, hon. How about just the two of us going out to dinner this evening? We don't do that very often, either."

"Sure. But not until eight or so, okay? Oz and I have some . . . homework . . . we have to get done."

"See you then," said Joyce. She walked off, then looked back. "Would you like to go to the new restaurant, The Laughing Greek?"

"Anywhere but there," said Buffy. "I'm allergic to figs. Or garlic. Or paintings of naked Olympians. Something."

"Oh, sure—right. We can choose when you get home. And maybe you'll have decided about the weekend?"

Buffy's jaw clenched, but she tried not to let it show. "Yeah, we can talk about it tonight."

"Okay."

"And by the way, you don't need to go into the basement, all right? I was down there working on a . . . project . . . and I left a really bad mess. I want to clean it up before you go down. Please?"

"Sure," said Joyce. She waved and went on. Buffy watched after her, then went to sit on the bench by the fountain to wait for Oz and Cordy.

CHAPTER 10

Xander had stayed home from school that day, as he'd promised Buffy, because for some reason he knew he was supposed to do what girls told him to do. When the school secretary called he said he didn't feel good, which was the truth, although he didn't really feel bad, either. He felt disoriented and numb.

And deep in his otherwise lethargic mind, he kept imagining the Moon sisters. How beautiful. How wonderful. How he would go looking for them as soon as he got permission to leave his house. How he wanted to be near them, even more than before.

Before what? his mind tried asking. But there was no answer. He couldn't think clearly.

He watched soaps most of the day, sacked out on the sofa with his sock feet drawn up beneath him and his head on a throw pillow. Then in the early afternoon he switched to Nickelodeon and watched kids' game shows, all of which seemed just about right for his frame of mind. He tried to fix himself some popcorn, but couldn't remember how to operate the microwave. So he lay back down on the sofa, shut his eyes, and let images of Polly and Calli drift through him like warm blood in his veins.

Until he heard a knock at the door. He sat up as quickly as he could—which was pretty darn slow—ambled across the living-room rug, nearly tripped on a corner of the carpet, and made it into the front hall. He tugged the door open. The late afternoon sun glared in his eyes, and he had to squint to see who was there.

It was Polly Moon.

It was his goddess in the flesh. Standing all alone on his front stoop, the sun forming a painfully beautiful aura around her painfully beautiful body.

"Hi, there," he managed.

"Good morning, Xander," said Polly with a toss of her long blond hair. "I want you to come with me."

"Sure," said Xander, not caring that he didn't have any shoes on. "Like where?"

"Oh," said Polly, reaching out to stroke his neck with her long painted fingernails. "Does it matter? Just wait and see. We have a little music to make, you and me."

"I'm really glad you're here for this," said Buffy to Oz as the two of them sat in the public library's computer lab, staring at the blinking cursor on an otherwise blank monitor. "I don't do computers. I kill vampires."

"I don't do computers, either," said Oz. "When I can help it."

"Yeah, sure, Mr. Techno-Whiz," said Buffy. "One of only two students recruited by that computer software company during Career Week. They didn't just do that because they liked your face, you know. Although you have a nice face—I'm not saying you don't. But you're talented with this stuff. I know it. You know it."

"I prefer music."

"So bite the bullet. Do it for Willow."

Oz took hold of the mouse.

It was almost five. The noisy middle schoolers who had been in the lab when Buffy and Oz arrived ten minutes before had gone, home for dinner Buffy assumed. She hoped. That way there could be some peace and quiet.

As Oz began mousing and clicking, Buffy's thoughts drifted briefly to her own middle-school days. Had she been as loud and obnoxious as those kids when she was thirteen? Oh yeah, she *had* been. Maybe even worse. She'd struggled with her body's changes. She'd grappled with an increased attraction to boys. And she'd wrestled with a confusing yet fierce *something* deep inside—something that made her feel she was walking around with the top layers of her skin shaved off, way too sensitive to people and experiences, uncomfortable just being alive. This, she had realized later, had just been her emerging Slayerhood. But it had also been—and still could be—yucky to the max.

"Where we heading with this?" asked Oz.

"Hypnosis. Of some kind. Bad hypnosis. As in not good."

More clicks.

A few wrinkled oldsters were on the other side of the room, pecking at keyboards and fussing at themselves for hitting occasional wrong keys. One old couple sat side by side on plastic chairs, laughing and sending e-mail. Maybe this couple was dating. Maybe they were in love. It was like watching middle schoolers, only these two had dentures and reading glasses.

"Hey Oz," said Buffy, looking away from the screen. "Do you remember middle school very well?"

"Yep. Hated it."

"Me too, but do you remember, like, realizing you were a guy and girls were girls? All that mess?"

Oz paused, grinning slightly. "I realized that in first grade."

"Yeah, I know but it's not until you start, well, changing physically that you really realize who you are. What you are. What you're turning into. Not counting the werewolf stuff. Just the guy stuff. What did you think being a guy was supposed to be all about?"

Oz shrugged. "We were pretty much expected to be athletic and strong. If we weren't, we were teased."

"Were you teased?"

"If I was, would I admit it?"

"I don't know," said Buffy with a smile. "Who did you think expected guys to be like that? Athletic and strong?"

"Parents. Teachers. Other kids. Television. Bruce Willis. 'Be a man. Don't cry. Don't show any emotion but anger.'"

"And what did you think girls were supposed to be?"

"Impressed by guys who didn't cry, guys who were athletic and strong."

"Oh. That's really wrong, though. Untrue and wrong."

"I don't believe it now," said Oz. "What did you think being a girl was all about?"

"Not that I ever exactly fit the mold, but a lot of girls tried to be flirty and popular in middle school. They were snotty about what they wore and put on way too much makeup. Some were already into giving boys exactly what the boys wanted in order to make the boys like them. Kinda sucked, but it happened. Such a freaking game, you know?"

"Like high school."

"Yeah. People don't grow up much, they just get taller."

"Your point?"

Buffy sighed. "The Moon sisters preach that to be female means to be all things, smart, musical, determined, and in control. I hardly know what it means to be Buffy Summers most of the time, much less the bearer of the title 'feminine.' Yeah, I still have stuffed animals in my bedroom, but I have a couple old Hot Wheels, too. I may freight-train my way through a batch of vampires like nobody else can, but I also like to cry at sad movies. Are there rules for being feminine and masculine? And if so, who made them up? Okay, the Moons are insane maniacal demonesses of destruction whose goal is total female rule in the high school and likely the whole town of Sunnydale and maybe even the world, but it's made me wonder about nature. How are things supposed to be? What is normal?"

Oz shrugged.

"I'm a Slayer. Slayers are females, from a long line of females. It makes for a strange family life. My mom has to pretty much ignore a lot of what I do. That's not normal for most families, but for Slayers it is. You change into a wolf each month. For most people that's really weird. For werewolves its normal. Or is it? How do we know what to change and what to leave alone?"

"Who knows?" said Oz. Buffy suddenly felt vulnerable, a sensation at once peaceful and troubling. Oz continued, "I think we should be whatever the best in us wants of us. But we don't have time to wonder. The Moons are dangerous. We have to stop them. That's all we should think about."

"Go ahead, Oz, get into it."

"Why don't you?"

"You're the boy. You're supposed to be smarter."

"You're the girl. You're supposed to be smarter."

They both laughed.

A web site on hypnosis linked them to animal magnetism, somnambulism, hallucinations, and psi phenomena. None of these links seemed to fit, because the Moon sisters never shut up, and hypnosis seemed to rely on concentration and a mode of quiet.

The next search took a while, as Oz tried to find information on the abnormal love of shiny objects. The only thing he found were painfully cute anecdotes about crows, raccoons, and monkeys refusing to let go of shiny things they'd retrieved at the risk of their lives.

And then a Greek tale about Atalanta, a young woman who lost a race and her freedom because she simply had to stop and pick up the shiny gold balls she passed along the way.

Buffy looked at the screen, reading and rereading the entry. She said, "The Moons meet at the Greek restaurant. Atalanta was a Greek chick. Do you think there's a connection here?"

"It's possible," said Oz. "Maybe one of the Moons is the ghost of Atalanta?"

Only in Sunnydale! Buffy frowned. "Maybe. There are three Moons and only one Atalanta. And what beef would Atalanta have with guys?"

"She did lose her race to a guy, and she had to marry him. Obviously she didn't want to."

"Right," said Buffy. Then she dug her fingers into her hair. "I wish Willow and Giles and Xander were here to help figure this out!"

"What time were you supposed to go out to dinner with your mom?"

"Eight."

"It's quarter after already."

"Great," said Buffy, jumping up.

"Can you call her? Cancel?"

"Not without major resentments on her part. There's a Mom-Dad competition brewing these days. I need to talk to her, to get it straight. I don't have the energy to walk in that quicksand right now, but I have to do something."

"Sure. No prob."

"Tomorrow, though. We can leave school during lunch again, so in the morning park your van where we'll have an easy getaway. We'll drive back here and nail this down. Then it'll be bye-bye Moons." She wasn't sure she was right. But sometimes saying things out loud made them seem more real.

Oz stood up and stretched. "Sure. Tomorrow afternoon. We'll be rid of old Palli and Colly."

"That's Polly and Calli. You sound like a college brochure."

"What's in a name?" quoted Oz. "A murderous, mind-controlling menace by any other name would smell as bad."

They walked out of the library and into the night.

On the way home in Oz's van, Buffy kept thinking, *What's in a name? I wonder? Could their names have anything to do with who they are?*

The hordes had gathered. Bodies were crammed together, as close as bees in a hive, buzzing and squirming. Emotions high, patience low. Hissing. Growling. Arguing.

Checking makeup. Kicking seat backs.

Gossiping. Snoring.

It was a second-period student assembly.

Principal Snyder had arranged for a sensitivity trainer

to speak to the Sunnydale High student body about "getting along." This morning, however, it seemed as if Principal Snyder had forgotten all about the assembly, or as if he didn't care anymore. He hadn't even come out of his office to introduce the speaker, so one of the teachers had to get up on stage to do it. She stood behind the podium and tapped the microphone for attention while the speaker stood near her, note cards in hand, a yee-hah string tie at his neck, and a hopeful expression on his face.

While the normally abnormal kids sat chewing knuckle skin or picking at scabs, a good sixth of the student body had found seats around the Moon sisters, surrounding them like worker bees around two queens. Allison and Willow sat to either side of the sisters. Anya was at the edge of the group, clearly still uncertain about them and right now looking less than impressed. The rest of the students glared at the group with anger, hate, and distrust radiating as surely as heat from a stovetop. Teachers stood in the aisles, some of them tense and watchful, others looking as though they had no idea why they were there or how they'd gotten there in the first place. Mo Moon was by the rear door, smiling.

Buffy sat with Oz and Cordelia in the back right corner of the auditorium. Cordelia was fidgety and furious; the fake potted plants so meticulously placed by the Miss Sunnydale High Pageant Committee all over the stage had been unceremoniously pushed aside for today's talk, and the sign she had helped paint for a backdrop—a big plyboard deal that read, "Sunnydale's Girls: They Walk in Beauty Like the Night"—had been temporarily shoved back into the chorus room. And to make things worse, word was out that Calli and Polly's pageant sponsors were W.B. Computers and Gameland of Sunnydale, both of which were, according to rumor, silent affiliates of Wayland Software Enterprises.

Buffy herself was in a foul mood. Last night, her twenty-five-minute tardiness had hurt her mother's feelings enough to cancel their girls' night out, and Buffy had eaten her cold-cut sandwich dinner to the tune of Joyce's silent treatment. They hadn't talked about anything, not even the pageant/hiking thing. Joyce had gone upstairs to her bedroom early, and before heading out for her nightly patrol, Buffy had checked on Giles in the basement. It had hurt her to see him like this. But she'd fed him a vegetarian taco and iced tea, fluffed the sleeping bags, and swore she was only doing what a Slayer had to do.

"Come with us during lunch," Buffy said to Cordy in the auditorium seat next to her. "Oz and I are going back to the public library to find a way to eclipse the Moons. We're getting close. We could use your help."

Cordelia raised one eyebrow. "We are *supposed* to have a Miss Sunnydale rehearsal this afternoon," she said. "That is, if they can manage to get the plants and the sign back in the right place. The pageant *is* this weekend."

"Is that a no?" asked Oz.

"Well, of *course* it is."

"Cordy, three heads are better than two," said Buffy. "You've helped us before."

"With some real half-baked ideas all your own," said Oz.

"Sorry, guys," Cordy said firmly. "Flattery won't work."

Buffy tried to stretch her legs out, but the seats were too close together. "I'm just glad Xander is staying home like I asked him," she said. "At least he's safe until this is over. It really makes me sick, thinking of him like that."

Oz nodded slowly. "Then there's Willow, sitting with the Moons, hanging on their every word. I wish I could make her safe, too."

"I know," said Buffy. There was nothing else to say. Not yet, anyway.

"Good morning, students," said the teacher on the stage. The microphone whined, and the teacher tapped it politely. "Today we are pleased to welcome Mr. Reilly O'Reilly to Sunnydale High School." There were snickers throughout the auditorium. The teacher continued. "Mr. Snyder has asked Mr. O'Reilly here in order to discuss the recent . . . quandary . . . in which we've found ourselves. We are a good school, with good students, good teachers, good administration . . ."

"And a real good mastery of adjectives," said Oz.

". . . and good facility and grounds. And so the tensions that have arisen between some of the female and male students has been troublesome. We know that young people often find it difficult to put differences aside and come to an understanding. That is why Mr. O'Reilly is here. He is a professional in the field of mediation and sensitivity enhancement."

The teacher indicated Mr. O'Reilly, and the man put his cards on the podium and took the microphone in hand. A boy in the audience yelled out, "Expel the Moon girls and let's get back to life as it was!"

"Ahem," said Mr. O'Reilly. He really said "ahem." Buffy never knew anybody to actually use that word, but he did, and it set off another wave of snickers across the room.

"Boys and girls," the man said, clutching the podium and leaning forward. "Adolescence is a time of conflicting feelings and confusing thoughts. I was once a teen like you. I understand. I'm your friend."

"Give us a break!" yelled a girl in the Moon group. "You don't have anything we need to hear! You're the man, trying to oppress the woman!"

"Excuse me, young lady?" said Mr. O'Reilly.

"That's womyn to you!" shouted the girl. "Spelled 'W-O-M-Y-N'!"

"Womyn power!" shouted the Moon following, getting to their feet and brandishing their T-shirts. "Womyn power!" The boys with them stood obediently and silently. In the center of it all, Polly and Calli smiled sweetly.

"Shut up, you mindless robots!" screamed the other students. Fists were shaking. So were voices. "You aren't taking over our school! We're sick of your attitudes!"

A girl leaped over her seat and grabbed a boy by the throat. Another boy caught a girl by the hair and tried to pull her up out of her seat.

Buffy nudged Oz and Cordelia firmly in the ribs. "Let's split. It's gonna blow." They hopped up and squeezed out of their seats and into the aisle.

A teacher they passed said, "Where do you think you're going? This assembly is for all students, not just some."

Buffy answered, "Cordelia's gonna hurl. We have to get her out of here—and fast!"

"Oh, I needed that for my reputation!" Cordelia wailed as they reached the end of the aisle.

The roar of the crowd lifted like an explosion behind them. Mr. O'Reilly could be heard over the din, but barely, begging the kids to sit down and think about ways to better express their anger.

Out in the hall, Buffy, Oz, and Cordelia paused to catch their breath. "If they tear up the auditorium," said Cordelia, "I'm going to be really upset! Where would the pageant be held then? The middle school? I don't think so. Their stage is really tiny, and a tiny stage makes the contestants look bigger." She grimaced.

"Who'd want to live?" asked Oz.

"Hey," Buffy said, lowering her voice, "we've got a little time while all that's going down inside. Let's get on the computer in the library. Nobody will miss us. I have a new idea on a lead."

"What kind of lead?" It was Mo Moon. She had followed them into the hall. Her eyes were bright and curious. The smile on her red lips was taunting.

Buffy tensed, but did her best to keep her voice even. "Government report. Current events. A lead on who might run for mayor next go-round. Mayor stuff. Important town stuff. Incredibly interesting. We thought, hey, there's this near-riot going on in the auditorium so it might be a good time for studious students such as ourselves to do some work while the tech lab's not so crowded."

Mama Moon walked up to Buffy, Oz, and Cordy. All three stepped back—and she noticed, but it only made her smile larger, colder. "You aren't going to work on a government project when you're supposed to be in assembly," she said. "And you aren't going to work on any other project, either. I know the students around here now. I know which ones are trustworthy, which ones aren't. I may have pretended for your mother, Buffy, but you and your friends are of the latter batch. You are in for a hard fall if you don't just take a deep breath and let nature take its course."

"Are you trying to make sense or something?" asked Cordelia.

And at that moment, the janitor came racing up the hallway, his face flushed, a mop gripped so tightly in his fist that Buffy swore she could hear the handle cracking.

"The pool!" coughed the man. "There's one in the pool!"

"One what?" asked Buffy.

"A boy. A dead boy! Drowned! With scratches all up and down his neck!"

God, no, not another one!

And Buffy was surprised to see the smile on Mo Moon's face fall, and an expression of anger take its place. "Oh, this is wonderful," the woman growled under her breath as she stalked off toward the office, her heels clicking, the janitor trotting behind. "Just wonderful."

"I thought you said the Moons were the ones doing the killings," said Oz. "So why would our wonderful library supervisor be upset?"

"I don't know," said Buffy.

"Forget that!" said Cordelia incredulously. "Did you check her shoes? That style heel is completely yesterday! What is *wrong* with that woman?"

CHAPTER 11

The police and paramedics arrived at Sunnydale High in wailing red-and-blue flashing vehicles in response to the near-riot in the auditorium and the body of Graham Edwards floating face-down in the pool.

The students had been herded outside, where they milled around, seeming a bit calmer in the fresh air, but still staring at each other as if it would take very little to get them at each other's throats again. Officers interviewed students to get their take on the riot, while Mr. Reilly O'Reilly sat inside a squad car, the door hanging open, fanning himself furiously with one of the "Can't We All Just Get Along?" brochures he had planned on handing out at the end of his speech and sputtering that this was unacceptable, this was the worst student behavior he'd ever encountered, Principal Snyder should just hang it up because these young hellions would never be sensitive if they lived to be 110.

Buffy, Oz, and Cordelia followed the ambulance around to the back of the school. Obviously, the paramedics and police didn't want the other students to see Graham's body being removed from the school, and thought the entrance through the custodian's office would be the best bet.

As if most students from Sunnydale had never seen a dead body before.

The three hid behind a row of azaleas, waiting for the crew to bring the body out. The red lights from the emergency vehicle pulsed in the air, a hypnotic, nauseating pulse that made Buffy shut her eyes for a moment.

"Buffy, help me . . . !" came the voice in her ear. *"Help me, help me!"*

I'm trying! Buffy opened her eyes defiantly. *I'm trying.*

"So just why did we come back here?" asked Cordelia, nudging her in the arm.

"I have to know if it's a Moon murder," said Buffy.

"And just how are you going to check?"

"You are going to distract them for me," said Buffy. "Being a distraction is one of your selling points."

"Oh," said Cordy. "Okay."

The wheeled stretcher came thumping through the door and down the short stretch of walk to the waiting ambulance. Two white-uniformed paramedics pushed the stretcher to the open back door, preparing to slide it in. The body lay obediently, silently, beneath the white sheet.

"Come with me," Cordy said to Buffy and Oz. She hopped up from behind the bushes. Buffy reached for her but it was too late. They hadn't even discussed a plan, and there went Cordelia. Hopefully, she wouldn't blow it.

"Oh, I'm *so* glad to see you!" said Cordy to the two paramedics, waving at them and trotting over to the ambulance. Oz and Buffy followed. "Excuse me, but I need to talk to you two for just a moment." She tossed her hair and scrunched her face. "I see you have your hands full there, but I know you guys are way good with medicine, aren't you?" She wrinkled her nose and raised one eyebrow. This, Buffy had to acknowledge, was one of Cordy's true talents. Getting guys to pay attention. At least initially.

"Sure," said one paramedic. He was no more than twenty, with dark hair and glasses. "We know all that stuff."

"Yeah," said the other one. He was also young, with red hair and a nervous tick in his right cheek. "But you aren't supposed to be back here. The police will—"

"I have, ah, a splinter," Cordy went on. "In my eye. It really hurts." She tipped her head and pointed one perfectly manicured nail.

"Yeah," said Buffy. "She could hardly see, so we had to bring her over here."

"Mmmm," said Oz.

"We can get it out," said the dark-haired man.

"But we have a body here," said the red-haired man. "Suspicious circumstances. We have to get to the morgue. These kids have to go back around . . ."

"Oh, owww," said Cordy, stamping a foot yet tossing her hair once again. "It really hurts, like a paper cut! It'll just take a second. Okay?"

"Please?" said Buffy. "We hate to see her in pain." *Too much,* Buffy added silently.

"Well . . . ," said the red-haired man.

"Over here." Cordelia went to the front of the ambulance. "Where there's more sun so you can see better."

"But let's first push this . . . ," began the dark-haired man.

"No!" cried Cordy, actually clutching his arm. "It hurts! Me first. That body's not going anywhere."

With a shrug, the men followed Cordelia around the side of the ambulance. As soon as they were out of the way, Buffy peeled back the top of the sheet, and hoisted the body up against the sunlit sky and stared into the eyes.

The brain was gone.

She dropped the body and Oz flung the sheet over it just as the paramedics came around the vehicle. Cordy followed, saying, "Look again! Look again!"

"If there's a splinter, I can't see it," said the dark-haired man.

"You should go to the doctor, let him have a look," said the other. "Sorry." Then he added, "But hey, you want to go to a movie tonight?"

Buffy inclined her head, indicating to Cordy that she'd seen what she needed to see. Cordy's helpless facade dropped like a ton of bricks. "Are you kidding?" she said with a sneer. "Hey, I like a medicine man as much as the next girl, but you are just not my type."

With that, she marched off. Buffy gave the paramedics an apologetic grin and said, "Gotta love her."

"Okay, let's give this another shot," said Buffy. She and Oz—and Cordelia this time—were back at the public library. It was just after noon. They'd escaped from Sunnydale High, picked up a fast-food lunch on the way, and—after telling the librarian they weren't skipping school because today was a teacher workday, didn't she know that?—settled themselves in front of one of the computers. Oz was at the keyboard; Buffy and Cordelia were on orange plastic chairs to either side of him.

Buffy pulled a folded sheet of notebook paper from her backpack. She read her notes. "The Moon family is very messed up and very powerful. They clearly want to establish an order of female rule in Sunnydale, beginning with the students and staff of the high school. The girls are doing some sort of mind-control of the students; the mother is mind-controlling the adults. They like to hang out at a Greek restaurant. They—at least the sisters—love gemstones to the point of complete and uncontrollable insaneness. And—one or more of them have killed at least four young men and turned their brains to Drano. Is that pretty much everything?"

Oz and Cordelia nodded.

"But Oz, you said something yesterday that stuck with me. Names. If Willow was helping, she'd have thought of this earlier. We often research demons by their names. We haven't even thought of going that route with the Moons."

"Calli? Polly? How odd is that?" asked Cordelia, crossing her legs and linking her fingers around her knees.

"Guess we'll find out one way or another."

Oz logged in, and Buffy said, "Try Moon."

Several sites came up, and in one entitled "Mystical Moon" they discovered several essays—one on lycanthropy, which made Oz roll his eyes, and another on the feminine principle and power represented by the cycles of the moon.

"Listen to this," said Buffy, leaning over Oz to have a better view of the screen. *"The moon is a symbol of the feminine principle, the occult side of nature, and all psychic phenomena, as well as the emotions, intuition, inspiration, imagination . . ."*

"Hey!" said Cordelia. "We're all that? Very cool."

"*. . . and the deep layers of the subconscious. It is a symbol of life, death, and rebirth as it waxes, wanes, and vanishes from the heavens and then reappears. The moon is considered to be the source of witches' power, and the moon itself is believed to cast spells which some label 'mania' or 'lunacy,' from the word 'luna,' meaning moon.*"

"Okay, okay," said Cordy. "So, the Moons are witches? Like Willow?"

Oz shrugged. "Let's keep going."

He typed in "Calli" and it brought up the word "calliope," with colorful artwork showing variations on the musical instrument.

"This is worthless," said Cordelia.

Oz clicked onto a link and said, "This might not be." He read from the screen, "*Calliope was the Greek Muse of epic poetry. She was one of nine Muses, lesser goddesses who, according to Greek mythology, were the inspiration for the arts and sciences.*"

"Yes, but—" began Cordelia.

"Wait," said Oz. He kept reading, "*The Muses were Calliope, epic poetry; Clio, history; Erato, erotic poetry and mime . . .*"

"Interesting combination," said Buffy. " 'Come on babe, I love you, so let's paint our faces and do a silent street act that annoys everybody.' "

"*. . . Euterpe, lyric poetry and music itself; Melpomene, tragic drama; Polyhymnia, sacred singing; Terpsichore, song and choral dancing; Thalia, comedic drama; and Urania, astronomy.*"

"Calli is Calliope," said Buffy, revelation at last dawning on her, "and Polly is Polyhymnia. It makes sense! Calli is known for her writing and Polly for her singing."

"So our demonesses are actually goddesses-es?" asked Cordelia.

"Looks that way," said Oz.

Buffy read on, *"The Muses were the daughters of Zeus and Mnemosyne, the goddess of memory."*

"Mnemosyne. Mo. Mo Moon," said Cordelia.

"Right," said Buffy. "And it says here they lived on Mt. Olympus and their leader was the god Apollo. I'm sure they just loved being told what to do by a god."

Oz pulled up another site on the Muses. "Check this out. Apollo never allowed the Muses to own any of the gifts of precious gems offered them by worshippers; he kept those for himself. *And they could not adorn themselves with sweet scents or oils, lest it detract from the purity of their task, that of enkindling the hearts of mankind."*

"Guess that's why they wear all that stinking perfume now," said Cordelia. "They were told they couldn't. Now they're going to do what they want."

"It also explains their obsession with jewelry," said Buffy. "They're making up for lost time. It doesn't say Mnemosyne wasn't allowed gifts, so that's probably why she doesn't seem concerned with diamonds and stuff like that."

They looked at each other, then back at the computer.

"Okay," said Buffy. "We know who they are. But we need more. A major kind of more. Like how do we get rid of them?" *We've never dealt with gods before,* she thought. *I could really use Giles's help!*

"I doubt we'll find that on the Internet," said Oz. "There may be sites dedicated to the occult and to killing monsters, but goddesses aren't typically thought of as monsters."

Buffy traded seats with Oz. She studied the information. There had to be something they could use. Surely they weren't going to be at the mercy of these deities forever. She simply would not allow it.

Then she saw it. "Here!" she said, tapping the screen. "Inspiration!"

Oz and Cordelia leaned closer.

"The Muses inspired humans to the arts and humanities," said Buffy. "This says that inspiration literally means 'breath.' Breathing the breath of the Moons from close in their vicinity has put the students and adults under their control! We've been okay because we don't let them get in our faces and breathe on us."

"Great!" said Cordelia. "So . . . how do we destroy them?"

"That I don't know," said Buffy, leaning back and stretching. Her shoulders and neck were sore. "They're quick and smart, and their wounds heal immediately. But there must be a way. Even Achilles had his fatal heel."

"I wonder what theirs is," muttered Oz.

Buffy stared at the screen until her vision went fuzzy. But the answer wasn't there.

He wondered when Mo would come for him. It had seemed a very long time indeed that he had been confined in this musty, subterranean, box-littered place waiting for her lovely face, warm smile, and sweet breath. She would come for him, he knew. She would not let him be alone much longer.

Giles lay on a pile of sleeping bags and gazed longingly out the grimy ground-level window. He could see the grass of a front yard, a row of staked rose bushes, the trunks of several trees, and squirrels darting about searching for sustenance. Sunlight played across the ground and filtered through the window glass to his face.

She was out there, somewhere. And she would find him. He was not afraid.

Buffy Summers had put him here, he knew that. She had tied his hands together, had lashed his knees together, and secured a gag in his mouth. She had said something to him—a reason for his confinement—but he couldn't remember what it was or if it made sense.

But it didn't really matter. Buffy didn't matter. Nothing did. The only thing that mattered was being with Mo, and doing what she asked of him.

Giles's dusty glasses had slipped on his nose, and he wrinkled it to push them back into place.

"Come for me," he mumbled into the towel gag. The words were garbled and unclear, but he knew she would hear. She would understand. She cared for him. She would help him.

Giles stared up at the window. The sunlight swelled, grew brighter, and then dimmed with the aging of the afternoon. But he waited. Patiently.

It was getting dark by the time Oz gave Cordelia a ride home, then Buffy. Buffy hopped out of the van, waved to Oz as he drove off down the road, and then started up the walk toward her house. *I'm going to decide tonight. Fashion show or camping. I'll just throw a dart at my choices and go with it. It'll be one less thing to think about. I'm sure Mom will—*

She froze.

And spun around, hair flying, hands pulling a stake from her pack.

But it was too late. Viva the vampire was on her, throwing her against a tree, hissing and snapping. The stake hurled through the air and skittered into the gutter. Buffy grunted, pulling her neck back as far as she could from the dripping fangs, then locked her legs around Viva's and with a quick twist, scissored the vampire to the ground on her back.

Viva was fast, and lashed out her arm to hook Buffy's own legs and pull them out from under her. Buffy slammed the vampire in the face with her fist, and they both fell at the same time. Buffy hopped to her feet.

"Cursed Slayer!" said the vampire. She kicked against the ground, gouging the earth and leaving scorch marks where her feet had dug. She sprang upward and faced her enemy.

"Don't take rejection well, do you?" chided Buffy. "Let me say it again. I don't like you. You smell and you're singularly unattractive. Sorry, girlfriend, but you'll have to accept the cold facts. We'll never be buds." With an explosion of energy, Buffy leaped into a flying side-kick, driving her foot into the vampire's face. Viva stumbled but stayed upright.

"Buffy?" came a voice from the kitchen window on the side of the house. "Are you out there?"

Mom, geez, just stay inside!

In the second she was thinking of her mother, Viva lunged forward, plowing into Buffy's chest. Buffy flew backward and landed hard, her head bouncing on the concrete sidewalk. Stars filled her vision, and then the face of the vampire. She rolled over and pushed herself to her knees.

Viva slammed into her again, grabbing one of Buffy's wrists and jerking it behind her. Buffy gasped in pain, and rolled into the arm to keep it from breaking. *That hurts!*

"Gotcha!" shrieked the vampire with glee. "And now you'll do what I tell you!"

With her free hand, Buffy reached out into the grass

by the walk for something, anything—and she found it. A stake protruding from the ground where her mother had tied up the new rose bushes. She yanked it free, cutting her hand on thorns from the young bush, then flipped over into her twisted arm, feeling the groan and sharp strain on the bone and muscle. But the agony immediately subsided, and she was sitting on the vampire, her knees in her chest, her feet planted squarely on the ghastly white arms, the smooth stick poised over the vampire's heart.

"Okay," she said, panting into the death-horrid face. "You have two choices. You can die slowly and oh so excruciatingly, or I can make it swift and relatively painless. Don't say I'm not a good sport."

Viva struggled and flashed her fangs, but Buffy's training and adrenaline were a formidable combination.

"If you want the swift death, you'll have to tell me some things I want to know. If you don't, then I can make this stake go in oh . . . so . . . slowly."

"They're trouble for both of us, you know!" spat Viva.

"So we *are* on the same wavelength," said Buffy. "The Moons. You know about the Moons. Tell me all you know."

"I don't know much."

Buffy pressed the stick. She could feel a slight parting of the skin beneath Viva's blouse. Viva grunted, snarled, and said, "Stop! All right!"

As Viva began to talk, Buffy found herself turning her face away. Muse breath might be dangerous, but vampire breath couldn't be a whole lot healthier.

"The Moon girls are two of the nine Muses," growled Viva. "Their mother is Mnemosyne, goddess of memory."

"Tell me what I already don't know!"

"Buffy?" came her mother's call.

"Be right in!" she shouted. And to Viva, "Talk!"

Viva's voice was tight with fury. "All right! I first met them in 1912. I was sired by a British vampire in Liverpool just days before I was scheduled to take a voyage on the new ocean liner, the *Titanic*. As a vampire, I decided I'd go anyway, since there'd be a pretty good-sized captive audience for my new appetite. Mo, Calli, and Polly were on the ship, too. I knew they weren't human right off. Vampires have the ability to tell a nonhuman from a human. Of course, they knew I wasn't human either."

"Yeah," said Buffy. "Coming out only at night and having big fangs and a corpse-like appearance is a bit of a giveaway."

"Whatever!" snapped Viva. "But Polly is the show-off of the three. She told me who they really were one evening, thinking there was nothing I could do about it. She laughed and said I might as well know who was going to take over the world before I died of starvation."

"Starvation? What do you mean?"

"I'm getting there!" said Viva. "Anyway, the Moons had been able to escape from the netherworld of Mt. Olympus because some museum curator was on the ship with a big collection of Greek artwork he was taking to America."

"So a concentration of Greek culture gave them the open portal they needed?" Buffy thought it through. "We have our concentration of culture—The Laughing Greek, such as it is. That and the Hellmouth allowed them to come to Sunnydale."

Viva bucked, and Buffy pushed the stick down harder. She stopped. "Yeah, right, right," she said. "So this is the deal. The Moons are incredibly hung up on having total female domination of the world. They'd had enough of Apollo telling them what to do and getting only minor recognition themselves. So they'd come to earth to establish a new order on Earth, with women in control and men completely subservient. It was a good time to do it, they figured, because in the early 1900s women's suffrage was a hot political issue. Women were ready to listen to them, ready for a big change."

"Ready to be breathed on and have their minds altered," countered Buffy.

"Breathed on by the daughters. Touched by the mother. That's how she makes adults so confused. She takes away their memories. So there they were, having the time of their lives, preaching women power and, in the case of Polly and Calli, snatching all the bright jewelry they could from the rich women on board. They'd planned on having the whole ship mind-altered by the time they got to the United States, and they would have had quite a nice little following to help them 'spread the word' from sea to shining sea."

"But . . ." began Buffy.

"But you saw the movie. The ship sank. The new order drowned or froze to death. In the panic of the sinking, everyone who had been enthralled by the Moon family forgot about them completely. Fear of death has a way of stripping the mind of everything else. Clears the head, so to speak. And since everyone forgot about the Moons at the very same time, they were sucked back to Mt. Olympus."

Buffy's mind was reeling. "So if everyone under their spell forgets them simultaneously, they'll be taken away?"

"Yes."

"I don't want them taken away. I want them dead. I don't want them to ever do this again!"

"I don't know how to kill them," admitted Viva.

Buffy took a deep breath, with her face to the side so she didn't get a huge whiff of vampire stink. "If this is all true," she said, "then why do you care if humans are controlled by these goddesses? I'd think you guys would get a kick out of a world full of zombies. The men especially would be easy targets."

Viva growled. Her face twitched. Her eyes pulsed with light. "Because," she said finally, "every human who has been mutated by the breath of the goddesses becomes poisonous to vampires. We can't allow them to spread their gospel because it ruins our food supply. You need them gone. We need them gone—"

"Viva!" It was a shriek, and it was close. Buffy looked over her shoulder to see two female vampires racing across the yard toward them, coats flapping wildly, mouths open to reveal caverns of sharp teeth. As one reached out her taloned hands for Buffy, Buffy spun about and jabbed the stick deep into the vampire's chest. The vampire went to dust and scattered into the grass.

But the shifting of her weight allowed Viva to pull free. She grabbed at Buffy's head but Buffy yanked away, leaving a hank of hair in the vampire's fingers. Scalp burning, Buffy dodged the grasp of the second of Viva's friends, rolling on the ground and grabbing the stick. She jabbed it upward into the demon. In a blowout of grit, she was history.

Buffy leaped up, waving the stick, and spun toward Viva.

But Viva was gone. Her form could be seen halfway down the street, running furiously.

Buffy leaned over to catch her breath. She spat on the

ground. Her scalp burned by her ear where some hair was gone. Luckily, she had plenty of hair and it would be easy to cover up. Her arm ached where it had been twisted, her shins were skinned, and her palms bruised.

And all on a school night.

"Buffy?" Joyce was at the front door now. "Aren't you ever going to come in?"

"Yes," panted Buffy. She limped toward the house, then saw movement at the basement window to the left of the porch.

She moved closer, across the grass, squinting down at the window.

His face was pressed there. Giles. The terrycloth gag was still in place, but she could read his words clearly though the expression in his wide, darting eyes. He understood. He wanted out. He wanted to help. It was the old Giles, back again.

Thank God!

Buffy ran up the porch steps and into the house. Joyce was in the kitchen, sipping a cup of coffee, the newspaper before her on the table. As Buffy pulled open the basement door, Joyce said, "You need to phone Xander's mother, hon. She called a short while ago and says she thinks he hasn't been home since yesterday."

Buffy's mouth dropped open. "She *thinks?*"

Joyce shrugged. "I always was under the impression there wasn't a whole lot of communication going on at the Harris house. But you know where he is, don't you? You guys are pretty tight, right?"

"Call Mrs. Harris for me!" said Buffy. "Tell her I'm going looking for Xander."

"But Buffy, don't you want to—?" Buffy didn't hear any more of what her mother had to say. She was racing down the basement steps and across the concrete floor to the pile of sleeping bags and her Watcher, standing at the window.

She yanked the gag from his mouth. Giles sputtered and cleared his throat. "Buffy," he managed. "I am so sorry. I don't know what happened to me, but whatever it was, it clearly made things more difficult for you. Having to put me in this . . . this crypt to keep me out of the way."

"Don't apologize," said Buffy. She quickly tore open the knots in the towels, and they fell from his arms and legs. "You couldn't help it. It was Mama Moon. She and her girls are renegade goddesses. They breathe on people. It messes them up, brainwashes them."

"I was looking out the window. I saw you fighting out on the lawn." Giles shook and the loosened binds fell free. He wiped his sleeve across his glasses. "I was mesmerized—*horrified*—seeing you in danger. Something inside me awakened. My training overrode whatever trance I was in, snapping me out of my fog, forcing me to focus on what was happening. I remembered my duty—your duty. But there was nothing I could do at the moment, bound up as I was—"

"But you can help me now. Xander's life is at stake!"

"All right, then," he said as they hurried through the basement and up the steps. "Where is he? What's the situation?"

"They haven't just been messing with people's minds, Giles," Buffy began, "they've been killing—"

Joyce was just outside the door, standing with her arms crossed, her forehead creased. Buffy nearly collided with her. "Um, Buffy," her mother said, "I didn't know Mr. Giles was with you. Was he—?"

"Came home with me, Mom," Buffy said. "We were looking for something in the basement. Couldn't find it. Think it's upstairs. Gotta go!"

Giles gave Joyce an apologetic smile. "Ah, good evening, Mrs. Summers . . . we'll chat later?" He followed Buffy to her room, taking three steps at a time with his long legs.

Buffy pulled open her closet door. Inside was an array of weapons she'd collected over the years for various species of monsters. "Help me," she told Giles. "What do you know about Greek mythology? How do I kill a goddess?"

Giles shook his head and rubbed his chin. "Well, this is a new one to me. The gods didn't die very much as I recall. They did fight, though. With spears, arrows, swords. This is not helping. Some supernatural Greek beings were drowned, stoned, eviscerated, or skinned alive. Medusa was beheaded."

"So my chances are as good with one as another," said Buffy. She crammed every weapon that would fit inside her backpack. She slung her crossbow over her shoulder. "Maybe I won't kill them, but I'll try. Regardless, I'm going to save Xander!"

Downstairs, Buffy told her mother she'd be back, then slammed through the front door. On her heels, Giles asked, "Where are you headed?"

"The Laughing Greek," said Buffy. "It's their hangout."

"I'll give you a ride." Giles turned, facing north on the street where his car had been parked the previous evening. "What? I've been towed!"

Buffy hit the road on foot, her legs pumping as fast as they ever had in her life.

"I'll just catch a cab!" called Giles.

Buffy reached the end of the block and turned west. Her heart pounded in her throat. Her arms were slick with a cold sweat. In her mind were images of Brian Andrews and Ben Rothman in their coffins, Adam Shoemaker lying dead by a puddle behind the football bleachers, and Graham Edwards on the stretcher by the ambulance, his eyes glazed, his skull empty.

No no no no no! she thought as she ran through the night. *Not Xander! I will not let you kill Xander!*

CHAPTER 12

Xander sat with his knees drawn up to his chin, unable to see anything but the slice of light coming from beneath the pantry door and the pale outlines of the cans and boxes on the shelves nearest the door. He didn't know how long he had been sitting there, but it felt like a long time. His butt was tired; his shoulders ached. He didn't know why he was supposed to be there, except that Polly had put him in there and told him he was not to make a sound because she would come back for him later. And that later they'd take a little walk to the beach. Where the water was.

Beyond the door, for what seemed like hours now, there had been chanting and singing and laughing. Women's voices. Correction—Womyn's voices. Polly Moon. Calli Moon. Their mother, Mo Moon. And their group of followers . . . friends.

Had he thought *followers?*

Were they followers? Did it matter? All that seemed to matter now was doing what he was told. Life was much easier that way, much sweeter. If he did what he was told, she would come visit him again. She would talk to him again. And her voice was otherworldly.

He closed his eyes and listened to the sounds outside in the main room of The Laughing Greek. No one had been in the restaurant when Polly had brought him there. The place had been empty except for the naked Olympians on the wall and the residual stink of bad cooking. Polly had had a key, and had said something about Mr. Gianakous turning the whole place over to them—the idiot, the fool, the typical male, hahahahahaha. And then at some point later—an hour? a day? years?—there were others, many others, some of whose voices he knew like Willow and Allison, others he did not know. But they were all female voices.

After a while, the music stopped. It sounded like they'd all gone away. Xander waited and listened. And listened.

And listened.

His nose itched . . . but it was hard to actually get his hand to obey the need to scratch it.

And then, suddenly, the door opened and the bright light from outside made him blink and gasp.

He couldn't make out the faces yet as his eyes adjusted, but he knew the voices.

Calli said, "Polly! Not again!"

Mo Moon said, "Curse you, daughter! I ought to put you on a slow boat to Hades! You have to stop this nonsense!"

And then Polly. Beautiful, sensuous Polly. "Mother, you simply don't understand."

"Oh, but I do," said Mo Moon. "I understand you are compelled to use your musical powers to kill males. But you also have to understand that Calli and I are sick to death of it. You need help. You need to find another avenue for your anger!"

Mo reached into the pantry and pulled Xander out to the hallway. He tried to keep his balance, but slammed into the wall. Stars swirled in his line of sight. Mo frowned at him as if he was something very distasteful. Calli had her hands on her hips. Polly looked at the floor, scowling.

"Polly," said Mo. "We are fed up to here with your grudge against human males. You have got to quit just killing them for fun. Where will we come up with adoring worshippers to do the menial tasks of our new order if you keep draining their brains?"

Polly shrugged and tossed her head. Blond hair fell like rain. Xander wanted to be buried in that hair. "I can't help it," she said. "I'm still mad at Neventine. My anger comes out in, well, inappropriate ways."

"Neventine was a worthless shepherd!" said Calli. "A human being. He slighted you 3,203 years ago. Get over it!"

"So it affected my feelings toward men," whined Polly. "And where is the problem with that? I've got residual anxiety, and I have to get rid of it *somehow*. It makes me feel better to kill a few males. You just don't understand or care about my feelings. No wonder the other seven decided to remain on Mt. Olympus. They were sick of your picking, picking, picking about every little thing, your incessant, constant criticism!"

"The other seven stayed back on Mt. Olympus because they have no vision," explained Mo, shaking her daughter by the shoulder. "They are content to tell stories, sing songs, and let that chauvinist Apollo tell them what to do and what not to do. I can't believe they are my children, Zeus have mercy. Such a disappointment.

At least you, my dears, are willing to make a stand for the eternal feminine."

"But you have to stop killing," said Calli. "Polly, are you listening? We don't need the extra hassle, okay? Jeez!"

"You sound like a mortal," said Mo. "Watch your mouth, daughter."

Polly ran her finger down Xander's neck. "Hmm? Oh, sure, yeah. No more killing. I'll try."

"I'm letting this one go," said Mo.

"Mother!" Polly stomped her foot.

Mo Moon took Xander by the hand and guided him through the dining room. He whacked his leg on several chairs, and it hurt . . . but it was too much effort to say, "Ow." Mo opened the front door and dragged him out to the sidewalk. "There you go," she said. "Now scamper home like all the other little boys. And stay away from Polly when she's alone. I know you find her more than just a little attractive, but I command you to just adore us from the periphery, like the other boys."

Then Xander heard a voice he hadn't heard in a while, coming from across the street. And for some reason, it was a comforting sound to him, something he knew he should be glad to be hearing. It was Buffy.

"There you are!" she shouted. "The Queen Lunatic and her miserable little Moon rocks. Get away from Xander! I'm here to take the three of you, and I'm not leaving until you're nothing but moon dust!"

Mo kicked Xander hard, and he landed on his face in the road. He managed to look up as Buffy strode past, her hands clutching myriad weapons, all sharp, all pointed, all very deadly. And even through his haze, he could see she was royally pissed.

* * *

She was alone with the Moons—well, except for Xander, who was not exactly there anyway. And she had clicked over into major war mode.

"Get across the street, Xander," she demanded.

"Stay there, Xander," said Polly.

Xander seemed to freeze where he was, unable to move now with the two commands.

"I know who you are, why you're here, and what you want," Buffy said as she stopped on the edge of the street, raised her crossbow to eye level, and trained the silver-tipped arrow on Mo Moon's chest. The fact that the woman . . . *the goddess demon* . . . didn't flinch made Buffy's heart tighten, but maybe it was a ruse to make her hesitate and wonder.

Let it be a ruse.

Buffy pulled the trigger. With a hiss and whack, the arrow went deep into the goddess. Mo shook her head and with a sigh, pushed the arrow all the way out the other side. It dropped to the sidewalk with a clatter, and she said, "You can't do it, Buffy. We know you are a special human, we've sensed that from the very beginning. But you can't kill us."

"Nobody can!" piped up Polly. "There's only one way to kill us and you'll never know what—"

Calli drove her open hand against Polly's face, causing her sister to squawk and stumble backward. "Would you ever learn to *be silent?*" she demanded. "We ought to have your tongue on a platter!"

Mo walked toward Buffy. Buffy hurled the crossbow away and pulled a machete from the pack on her back. This had never been good with vampires, but there had been plenty of demons who'd found it a disarming bit of steel. She waved it threateningly at the library supervisor. "You can die," she said evenly. "Everything can die."

Mo laughed shrilly, and snatched for the machete. Buffy whipped it back out of the goddess's reach, then with an agile spin and leap whirled it up, around, and down into Mo's skull. It cut clear to the bridge of the nose, and hung there, wavering with the force.

Mo stopped in her tracks. Her mouth dropped open. Her eyes, now parted from each other by the gap in her head, looked upward toward the night sky in eerily different directions. Buffy felt a surge of hope. *Yes, that was it, like that* Night of the Living Dead *movie—kill the brain, kill the ghoul.*

But then Mo began to laugh, and with both hands, she forced the blade up and out of her head and let it fall to the ground.

No!

"Come here, Buffy," said Mo, as the grisly split in her face drew up with a soft sucking sound, like an obscene Zip-loc lunch bag sealing shut, until there was no sign she'd ever been whacked. "Why be adversarial, Buffy? If you just see it our way, you'll understand that we mean only for the best. We mean to raise women to the highest level ever attained."

"With you in charge, and males reduced to gibbering idiots—I don't think so!"

Polly and Calli had begun circling around on either side of Buffy, their arms stretched out, huge smiles on their oh-so-pretty faces. All they needed to do was to grab her, hold her for a matter of seconds, and breathe in her face. Buffy waved the hatchet she'd pulled from her pack, for all the good it would do her.

They have to die somehow! she thought. *There has to be some weakness! I wish Angel was back! I could use another pair of hands!*

"You can be part of it, part of us," said Calli. "Not immortal, of course, but think of the *power!*"

With graceful side steps, the three continued around Buffy until they formed a triangle in which she was trapped. The breeze that had been blowing down the street subsided; the air was momentarily still and stagnant. Buffy knew that if the Moons were able to close in on her and breathe on her at close range, she was as good as brain-dead.

Like Willow. Like Xander. Buffy's heart clenched at the thought yet again, and yet again it fired fury in her soul.

"Join us before Friday night," said Polly with a giggle. "Before the Miss Sunnydale High Pageant. We're going to cram as many people as we can into the auditorium. Then during the first musical number we're going to lock the doors and start breathing right on them, and in those tight quarters . . ."

Calli spun on her toe and pounced on her sister, grabbing her flowing hair and yanking her hard. Polly pinwheeled her arms and stayed upright. "Would you *ever* learn to shut up and stop showing off?" Calli screamed. "You are such a moron! Such a big mouth!"

"Daughters! Daughters!" said Mo, pointing a finger at Buffy. "Task at hand! Task at hand!"

But Buffy's task at hand was in her hand. She charged Mo with the hatchet, screaming like a soldier in battle. Perhaps a split head wouldn't do it, but a severed head? Hadn't Giles mentioned Medusa? Mo reached out her arms to block the attack, and thrust out a leg to trip the Slayer. But Buffy dodged the leg and the arms, dipping down to the right and then swinging the hatchet up toward the neck. Mo shielded herself with her arm, an expression of tolerant patience on her face, and the hatchet went through the forearm and the neck in one quick succession. Both the arm and the head popped off and rolled down the street. The head rolled better.

The head lay blinking on the tarmac. "Buffy, Buffy, Buffy," it said. "You just don't understand, do you?" The fingers on the disembodied hand scrabbled in the gravel. The headless body, still upright, reached down, snatched up the pieces, dusted them off, and put them back into place. Immediately, they healed back.

Buffy's mouth fell open. This was a new one. This was a way bad, way disturbing, way unnerving new one. Calli and Polly had quit their arguing to watch the assault on their mother, and now were approaching Buffy again.

"Come on, Buffy," they said, reaching out their hands toward her.

"Come on, Buffy," said Mo with her insipid smile. "We need you, you need us, Womyn power!"

"Womyn power!" said Polly and Calli.

Buffy had never been one to run from a fight. She had a job to do, and jobs didn't get done by hot-footing it in the opposite direction. But her mind was already telling her that escape might be the only recourse. *I can't kill them!* her mind cried. *What else can I do?*

But then she saw she wouldn't have to run. Oz's van was hurtling down the street toward her, the headlights cutting the night air like twin beacons from heaven. Buffy jumped out of the way, and the vehicle slammed into Polly and Calli, sending them flying like goddess Frisbees. They laughed as they hit the ground, then hopped to their feet and ran for the van. The van door popped open. Oz shouted, "Get in get in get in!" and with Xander in tow Buffy crawled in as fast as she could and slammed the door shut. Calli's middle finger was caught in the door, and came off inside. It twitched like a worm. Buffy kicked it away. Xander stared at it as if it was a cherished relic.

Oz jammed the shift into gear, and with Mo Moon pounding on the windshield glass, punched the gas pedal. Mo fell away, and in a matter of moments, the van was around the corner and heading for home.

Buffy sat still, trying to catch her breath. She put one arm around Xander protectively and said, "I was this close, Oz, *this* close. Xander could have been . . ."

"But he wasn't," said Oz. "You did good. Giles called me from your house right after you left, saying you were heading for The Laughing Greek and might need back-up."

Buffy nodded. She looked at the finger up against the door. It was no longer moving. She wondered how Calli would explain the missing digit come school tomorrow. Maybe it would be like that movie she'd rented once, *The World According to Garp,* where the cult followers cut out their tongues to honor their icon. Maybe the Moon followers would start chopping off their own fingers to fit in.

Buffy shivered violently.

"Oz," she said as they pulled onto Buffy's street, "could Xander stay at your house? Could you call his mother and tell her? She doesn't seem real tuned in to Xander's comings and goings, and I need someone who can watch him until this is all over."

"Sure," said Oz, but he drew the word out long, as if he was wondering if this would all ever really *be* over.

"Sure," said Xander softly.

Buffy held him tightly and tried not to cry.

* * *

Willow isn't much of a witch, Buffy thought as she pulled herself up her walkway to her front porch. *But she's written some spells down for me and I've stuck them in my desk upstairs. Maybe there's something in all of that scribbling I can use against the Moons. Generic attacks are certainly worthless. If only Willow were here to help me.* She opened the front door, knowing Willow-spells were such a sad stretch. *If only . . .*

There was big-time tension brewing inside the Summers household. Joyce was on the phone. And Buffy didn't have to reach far to guess with whom. Her father.

She walked into the front room and stood, staring in the direction of the kitchen, where the noise was coming from. *This is so totally wrong,* she thought. *Such a waste of time! Arguing over me when there is something really critical going on!*

"I don't know where she is, Hank!" came Joyce's voice. "She just ran out and . . . yes, I know you want to talk to her, but she's so busy and . . . wait, wait . . . Hank, I'll have her call you, what else can I do? No, I have no idea what she wants to do this weekend, she hasn't said yet. We've talked about it on several occasions but she hasn't decided . . . Hank, would you just—Hank?"

Buffy walked into the kitchen.

"Buffy, there you are!" said her mother, her hand over the mouthpiece. "Are you okay? Did you find Xander?"

Buffy nodded slowly.

"Is he all right? I was so worried!"

She nodded again. Her nerves were scratching inside her skin. All she needed was one more thing to deal with tonight.

"Will you please talk to your dad?" Joyce asked, handing the phone out in Buffy's direction. "He really needs to know what you want to—"

Buffy blew up. "I don't want to do either! I'm sick of this mess! I've become a pawn for you two, and I've never been that before! Don't you hear yourselves? Don't you see yourselves? I have more things to worry about than whose feelings I'm going to hurt over a ridiculous, worthless weekend! Do you have any clue how hard my life is right now, and I have to listen to your matriarch-patriarch power struggle over something as stupid as me?"

"Oh, Buffy," said Joyce. Over the line, in a tiny, tinny voice, Hank said, "Oh, honey."

Joyce said, "Hank, let me call you back, okay? Just a few minutes." She hung up, and turned to Buffy.

Buffy leaned back against the kitchen wall and put her hand over her face. She took deep, cleansing breaths like Giles had taught her to do when things seemed overwhelming. She felt so totally defeated. Every aspect of her life seemed turned on end.

"Buffy," said Joyce softly, her voice shaky as if she had begun to cry. "Look at me."

"My eyes hurt," said Buffy. She didn't want to see her mom crying.

"Then listen to me."

"Okay."

Her mother began stroking her hair. It felt good, calming. "Buffy, your father and I didn't realize what we were doing to you. We didn't know the pressure we were putting on you. We got into our own little tug-of-war and didn't see the consequences. I'm so sorry."

Buffy nodded, but didn't open her eyes.

"Honey," said her mother. "You are my breath of fresh air each morning. You are more important to me than my own life, and I never, ever want to do something like that to you again."

Slowly, Buffy opened her eyes. She smiled at her mother and gave her a hug. *Yes,* she thought.

Yes!

"Thanks, Mom," she said.

Her mother had said some very kind things. But her mother had also given her the answer to how to kill the Moons, once and for all. She went upstairs, called Giles and Oz, and gave them the news.

CHAPTER 13

"Now give that to me again," said Cordelia to Buffy at lunch on Friday. She wasn't eating anything today. She said she wasn't hungry, but Buffy knew pre-pageant jitters when she saw them. "How exactly do you kill them?"

Buffy took a deep breath and repeated herself, keeping her voice at a near-whisper. "It all has to do with focus. Viva said that for the Moons to be returned to Mt. Olympus, everyone under their influence has to forget about them at the very same time. That's rather hard to do, but I don't want to merely send them home, I want them gone for good, never to return."

"And that means two different things—one for the daughters, one for the mother," said Oz. He had understood Buffy's explanation the first go-round. Of course, this was Cordelia they were talking to. "The daughters have to have their breath sucked away. This is their essence, their purpose for existence."

"And Mo Moon, the goddess of memory, has to forget

about her own self. In that moment, she will be totally vulnerable," added Buffy.

"Hmmm," said Cordelia. "And you figured this out how?"

"Something that happened to Giles in my basement," said Buffy. "And something my mother said to me last night."

"And now that you've had this revelation," said Cordy, "how exactly do we go about sucking breath from two Muses and making the goddess of memory forget herself?"

"Believe it or not," said Buffy, leaning on the table and staring down at the fruit salad, which was staring back at her with seedy, strawberry eyes, "I've got it figured out." *I think I have it figured out,* she thought. *I better have it figured out.*

On the way to class after lunch, Cordy, Oz, and Buffy stopped by the auditorium to see the progress on the decorations for the Miss Sunnydale High Pageant, which would be held in less than eight hours. Anya passed them in the hall, then came back to stand beside them and gaze into the large room. Her face was drawn up and disgusted.

"I thought you would have entered the pageant," Buffy said to Anya. "Weren't you digging the Moons' rhetoric? They really seem your type."

Anya shook her head. "They're lame. We went to The Laughing Greek that night? And I began mentioning to them all the great ways to get rid of bad men? They just cackled like some crazy old hens. Wusses! I left them standing there. I'll have my own club of one, thank you very much. Hey, where's Xander? I've missed him the past few days."

"Home with the flu," said Buffy. She turned her attention back to the goings-on inside the auditorium. Anya strutted off.

The three Moons, of course, were now in charge of the decoration committee. Snapping their goddess fingers, they directed their followers to hang bunting, replace the potted plants, and situate bright red begonias on white stands to either side of the "Sunnydale Pageant" sign upstage. All the goddesses were snapping except Calli, that is, who was missing her middle, snapping finger. Buffy had noticed, however, that a new, stubby replacement had already begun to grow in its place. None of the followers seemed to care. Allison, all smiles, was up on a ladder, hanging paper flowers on the curtains. Willow was at the bottom of the ladder, holding it for her new best friend.

"Actually looks pretty nice," admitted Cordelia.

"These are Muses we're talking about," said Buffy. "They are supposed to be the Big Kahuna when it comes to the arts. They better be able to plan a nice-looking pageant or what good are they?"

"Some parents aren't letting their daughters participate tonight," said Cordy. "Some have even called the mayor to ask that it be postponed because of a rumor that some boys are going to crash the pageant, since they weren't invited. All I can say is they better not mess with the pageant. I've bought a floral bikini for the trip to Hawaii, and I will not be disappointed!"

"With luck," said Buffy, "the *pageant* will go off without a hitch."

It was a long day. After school let out, Buffy stopped by the mall for some supplies, then went home, made some quick preparations, then tried to rest. Tonight was the night it had to happen. If not tonight, then never. And

Sunnydale would be at the mercy of the Moons, without recourse.

Without challenge.

Before returning to school at six-thirty, Buffy called her mom at the gallery, where she was working late.

"Hey," she said.

"Hey, honey," said her mother. "How was your day?"

"Okay," said Buffy. "I'm really sorry I can't do the fashion-show thing with you tonight. I hope you aren't too terribly disappointed. Sometimes recently I feel that is all I can do. Disappoint people."

"Never," said Joyce. "I'm never disappointed with you."

"I called Dad and left a message on his voice mail," Buffy said. "I apologized for being difficult. I promised that I'd hike with him next time he gets a cabin."

"That's good."

"I love you, Mom."

"I love you too, hon."

She hung up the phone, called Oz to finalize the plans, and headed back to school in the dwindling daylight.

Cordelia—dressed in a sleek emerald-green floor-length gown—caught Buffy in the hall outside the auditorium. All around them parents, grandparents, siblings, friends, and reporters were filing in, talking nervously, some about their daughters' and granddaughters' chances at a prize, others about the gathering outside on the walkway.

"Did you see the boys out in front of the school?" Cordy asked, clutching at Buffy's sleeve. "They have posters and everything. 'Men Power!' 'Ban the Moons!' 'Males Deserve the Runway!' They are going to ruin the pageant, I just know it. They're going to come in right in the middle and make a big scene! Probably during my dramatic reading!"

"Keep calm," said Buffy. "If you help me, everything should be back to normal in a matter of just a few hours."

"Yeah, you told me that," said Cordelia. "But I have to be onstage for the opening number, remember? And I'm number thirteen to do my talent act. I absolutely won't be late."

"I only need you for a short time, Cordy. Chill."

"So where is Oz?"

"Down at the pool with Giles. I told you. They've got their jobs, we have ours. Now go inside and get ready for the pageant. When the opening number's done, meet me back here. Right away."

Cordelia nodded reluctantly. Then she let herself be swept up in the human flood pouring into the auditorium.

Buffy went to the front door of the school and looked out. Most of those who had come to attend were now inside, taking their seats. A few stragglers trotted up the walkway as best they could in heels and slippery wing-tip shoes, through the shouting gauntlet formed by the protesters. This would make tomorrow's newspaper as easily as the winners of the pageant.

At least if Buffy had her way, and was able to nip the Moons' buds so they couldn't pull off that breathe-on-everyone-in-the-auditorium-and-make-them-ours-ours-OURS stunt Polly had let slip the other night during the fight. Because if that did happen, nobody would much care about pageant winners, protesters, or even whether the sun would rise or set. All they would care about would be doing the bidding of their goddesses.

I won't let it come to that, Buffy thought. *I'm the*

Slayer. I'm the Slayer. I'm the Slayer. The mantra helped a little, but still her nerves were raw and on edge.

She went back to the auditorium and stepped inside the door, letting it ease shut silently. Polly and Calli Moon were sitting in back seats, dressed in identical sparkly silver gowns, ridiculous tiaras in their perfectly curled blond hair. They should have been behind the stage with the other contestants, preparing for the opening routine, the painfully pleasant "Miss Sunnydale High" theme song and the dance number honoring Wayland Software Enterprises. But it was clear there was something the sisters had to do first.

Mo Moon walked onstage to welcome the audience. She was dressed to the hilt, in a gold spangled gown with a beaded jacket. She thanked everyone for coming out on a Friday evening, recognized Wayland officials for their kind generosity and the Sunnydale Small Business Association representatives for the fashion show that would be held during intermission, and congratulated the parents of the contestants on girls well raised.

Then she said, "I'd like someone to go outside and invite in all those poor boys who are holding those silly signs. Such a pity, to be so full of anger. Yes?" Mild applause rippled across the crowd. Calli and Polly folded their hands smugly in their laps, watching it happen. "Let us invite them to watch. And if, by the time the show is over, they still feel they have bones to pick with those of us of the feminine persuasion, then I shall let them have the stage. We shall sit and hear their complaints without interruption or dissent. Is that fair enough?"

More applause.

That's the plan, Buffy thought. *When the boys come*

in, the room will be full. Shut doors, shut windows. Stale air. Then the big-time breathing session will begin.

"Calli? Polly?" said Mo Moon through the mike. "Would you please go outside and invite those boys to come in and see what we are all about?"

Calli and Polly hopped up and went out the door. As Buffy followed, she could hear Mama Moon begin introducing the judges.

Buffy hid beside the trophy display case while the boys came marching in from outside, their faces set and their hands still clenched around their signs. They'd taken the offer. Little did they know what the offer might entail. Buffy quickly rolled out the first part of the trap. Polly held the auditorium door open and the boys filed through. It was then that Calli spied the diamonaire on the floor, one of a heap of gems Buffy had bought that afternoon at the mall with every penny she had to her name.

"Oh," she said, pulling on Polly's sleeve and pointing.

The auditorium door shut with a soft click. Boys inside, Moon girls out in the hall. Looking with rapture at the sparkling, real-looking gems.

Oh please oh please oh please, Buffy thought.

They began snatching up the stones.

Buffy hurried down the hall, staying in doorways and out of sight, dropping more sparkling lures in a trail that would lead the girls to where Buffy wanted them. Polly and Calli were quick, keeping up. Cordelia had worried that Mo Moon would immediately suspect something was wrong if her girls weren't back to do the opening number, but Buffy was certain that Mo would be anything but worried. She'd assume her daughters were chasing up a few more unsuspecting folks to bring into the hall of death. Besides, being in the pageant wasn't the real goal, anyway.

The real goal was total domination of the human race.

Buffy dropped a few stones at a time down the stairs that led to the swimming pool. She eased open the door to the steamy room and rolled a few more across the tile floor and into the pool. Then she hid with Oz and Giles behind the stack of plastic chairs used by the judges at aquatic events.

"Are they on their way?" whispered Giles.

"Yeah. You crack it?"

Oz nodded. "Turned off the pump and hit it with a brick, as good as I could underwater, that is. Pump's back on now."

"Good," said Buffy. Her heart was pounding madly. She touched Oz and Giles's hands briefly for luck. Oz's hand was holding the end of a length of wire, which also ran across the floor and into the deep end of the pool.

The door burst open. "More!" said Polly. She and Calli scrambled across the tile, their well-polished fingers making little scratching sounds as they scooped up their irresistible bounty, their tiaras bobbing on their heads at the ends of loose hairpins.

Then the girls stood and stared with awe into the water. It was here that the most tempting lure of all had been placed. Four strands of glistening pseudo-gems—rubies, emeralds, sapphires, amethysts, diamonds, topazes—all lying on top of the drainhole cover, looking like alms worthy of a goddess or two.

Temptation is a funny thing. It can make people do all sorts of things they might not do otherwise. And it can make lesser deities dive into a pool with pageant gowns and tiaras on.

And dive they did. Well, not exactly dive, because Muses weren't classically trained swimmers, but they were obviously comfortable enough with water to venture down to ten feet below in order to grab the objects of their desire.

Buffy ran to the edge of the pool, her hand held up to give the signal. Down below the surface of the water, their blond hair and silver gowns billowing, the sisters clawed at the strands of gems, at first gently, then with increasing fury.

Oz had tied the strands of gems to the edge of the drainhole cover he'd cracked.

And he'd tied the end of the wire to the cracked cover as well, ready to yank it free with all his might.

Calli and Polly had lost their patience. Their legs paddling furiously to keep them at the bottom of the pool, they snatched at the gems. And then, at the moment that both of their faces were directly over the drainhole cover, Buffy shouted, "Now!"

Oz pulled the wire with a howl of determination. Buffy heard him fall over, knocking plastic chairs everywhere. And then she saw the cracked piece of cover come free for the barest moment, but just long enough for the Moon sisters' faces to be pulled to the hole with the dreadful force of the suction. They were pinned there, flapping their arms desperately in an attempt to escape as the force sucked and sucked and *sucked* their breath through their mouths and out of their lungs.

"Is it working?" called Oz as he clambered from beneath the pile of chairs and hurried to poolside with one of the scoop nets used to get things out of the water. Giles was beside him, pool steam clouding his glasses. "Oh, yeah, guess so."

Giles wiped his lenses. "That's rather unappetizing, isn't it?"

"Yeah," said Buffy. "Sure is."

The Moons' arms and legs battled the water, churning

a violent undertow. They scratched at the pool floor, at each other, seeking release from the hold. And then their struggles grew weak. And weaker. Then they stopped altogether. With their mouths still pinned to the drain hole, the Muses' lifeless bodies went still. Their arms drifted to their sides. Their tiaras landed on the pool bottom with a soundless clunk.

"Turn off the pump," said Buffy, taking the scoop net. "They're dead."

"Okay," said Oz. "Two down. One to go."

Cordelia made it back out into the hall on time, amazingly. She looked harried, though, and still put out that she was at risk of being late for her own talent performance. "Willow's talent—a computer demonstration, of all things—is next. Then Allison is going to cook something with a microwave easy-bake oven, some kind of food-preparing thing. Then comes Ashley with her flute, and I'm after that! So!" She put her hands on her hips. "What do I do? Quickly!"

Buffy handed her the Moon sisters' tiaras and said, "Take these backstage and give them to Mama Moon. Tell her I'm out here waiting for her, and that there is something she must see for herself."

"That's *it?*"

"Do you want it to be more?"

"Well, no, of course not, but this is kind of nothing."

"Just do it, Cordy."

Cordelia blew a noisy breath of air through her teeth, slid the tiaras over her wrist, and slipped back into the auditorium. Buffy could hear a piano tune being played inside. A talent performance. Buffy waited, taking deep breaths, bringing her mind back to the chore she had yet to accomplish. Polly and Calli were dead. Their inspiration had been taken away, stolen from them, and they were no longer. Mama Moon, however, was the biggest gamble. Buffy thought her theory was right, but knew that if it wasn't, there would be Hades to pay.

And then some.

The auditorium door slammed open. Mo Moon stood there, eyes ablaze, glaring at Buffy, holding the tiaras. Her question was simple and to the point. "Where are my daughters?"

"Wouldn't you like to know?" replied Buffy evenly.

"I'll make it easy," said Mo, striding close to Buffy. "Something simple for you to comprehend. If you do not take me to my daughters immediately, I will kill you."

Buffy skipped backward. "If you kill me, you won't ever know where Calli and Polly are. How simple is that?"

"You play with me, you . . . *human?*" demanded Mo.

"It's what I'm good at!"

"I thought you'd seen clearly what it is you are up against. And yet you are still under the misguided impression that you have some sort of *power* over us? That you can do anything to stop us in our quest for the new order? It would be sad, were it not so pathetic!" She lashed out at Buffy, but Buffy jumped back.

"Go ahead, catch me and kill me if you can, Mnemosyne," said Buffy. "You won't find Calliope or Polyhymnia!"

"But I will," said Mo. "You underestimate me! We do not die, but you mortals do—and I can make it excruciating! Then, when you are out of the way, I'll find the silly little place in which you've temporarily detained my girls, and we'll laugh about you when all's said and done!"

"Laugh and breathe on all those unsuspecting souls in the auditorium?"

Mo nodded. "It's what we're here for."

"But you won't be here much longer!" Buffy wiggled her head and laughed. Mo snarled, sounding a whole lot like a vampire at that moment. Buffy danced in and slapped the goddess on the face, then turned and ran down the hall toward the library. "Catch me, you goddess of memory!" she yelled. "Or is your memory failing—and you've forgotten how much quicker I am than you!"

She could hear the goddess thundering after her. The deity was faster than Buffy would have guessed. *Maybe back in the old days she'd had a little training from Mercury—or rather Hermes, Mercury's Greek opposite number . . .* If she actually reached Buffy before they made it into the library . . .

Buffy slammed into the library door, then yanked it open, panting, yelling, "Oz, Giles! We're here!"

And then a hand grabbed the back of her collar and hurled her away from the door with a single, effortless motion. Buffy hit the wall on the other side of the hall, but forced herself upward to face the goddess. The lovely library supervisor had lost a bit of her beauty. In fact, she looked more like the snake-haired Medusa than sweet inspiration.

"Die, you worthless mortal!" screamed Mo. She dove on Buffy, grabbing around her neck as if to snap it in two. Buffy arched her back and jabbed her elbow into Mo's ribs. But the goddess didn't feel it. Impervious to wounds. Immune to pain.

Buffy wrenched back and forth, tugging with all her might, until her head at last slipped through Mo's grasp. She jumped up, kicked the goddess for good measure, and ran into the library. She skidded to a halt at the bottom of the steps.

And so did Mo Moon.

The expression on the goddess changed from rage to utter disbelief.

"Hey, we found 'em!" said Buffy, pointing.

There, tied in an upright position against the bookshelves on the upper tier, were Calli and Polly. Their clothes were drenched with pool water, their eyes glazed, their faces flattened.

"But we forgot to tell you something," said Giles from beside the bookshelves.

"They're dead," said Oz, standing by Giles.

Mo's mouth fell open. Her eyes widened and twitched. For the first time in her entire existence, the goddess of memory forgot about herself completely. She was caught in the supreme grief of seeing her children dead.

Mo fell to her knees, still staring at her daughters. She lifted her hands to the heavens, and with a violent shudder, she cried out. And then it was as if every cell in her body joined the chorus of anguish. The sound emanating from the goddess was a tortured Greek chorus of screams and screeches—discordant, ear-splitting—that rose to the ceiling like the spirits of the damned.

"Apollo!" Mo cried. "Zeus! No!"

She folded over, clutching her face in her hands. And in that one completely vulnerable moment, Buffy drew a single vampire stake from her pocket and impaled the goddess through the back. Mama Moon fell over, gasped, and died.

Buffy's arms dropped to her side. She stared at the mother on the floor, for she was nothing but a dead mother now, a parent who had seen her children killed. A parent who loved her children.

Then all three bodies flickered and vanished, leaving no trace.

"It worked," said Oz simply.

"Yeah," said Buffy. "It sure did."

Through the library window, Buffy heard a shrill cheer. She looked up to see Viva's grinning, ugly vampire's face pressed to the glass. A shiver coursed through Buffy's body. She had rid Sunnydale of the Moons' threat, but she had also saved the vampires.

Where's the justice?

"So, have we just brought the wrath of Mt. Olympus's gods and goddesses down on our heads for all this?" asked Oz.

Buffy shook her head uncertainly. "I got the feeling that Mo, Polly, and Calli were sort of on the outs with Zeus and his gang. That they were the bad apples, not playing by the divine rules. Of course, here in Sunnydale—who knows?"

"Who knows, indeed," mused Giles.

"Wanna watch the rest of the pageant?" asked Oz. "I've put two dollars down on Ashley Malcolm to win."

"Who's place and show?" asked Giles with a weary smile.

"Why don't we go and see?" said Buffy. "I bet the air's pretty fresh in there now." She linked her arms through Oz's and Giles's, and they walked out.

The Bronze was filling up with the after-pageant crowd. Buffy, Oz, Cordelia, and Willow stood just outside the door, recapping the evening's activities. Everyone who had been mind-altered by the Moons seemed to be back to normal, with very little recall of what they'd been through over the past few weeks.

"I'm really happy Allison won the crown!" said Willow. She was holding Oz's hand tightly, as if she never wanted to let go. Oz looked more than happy about it. "She really is pretty, we just didn't see that at first. And go figure—turns out she can cook like a dream! I'm sure her father will be glad of that. And she gets to go to Hawaii and everything!"

Cordelia's eyes were slits. The skin beneath her nose twitched. "Allison won first place!" she hissed. "And I got first runner-up! Wrong much? Totally inept judging much?"

"But Cordy," said Willow. "You got a great prize, too. You won a brand-new set of encyclopedias!"

Cordy threw up her hands and stormed into The Bronze. Oz and Willow chuckled and followed her inside. Buffy stood out on the gravel until everyone else had entered, then looked up at the distant half-moon and remembered what Oz had said to her.

I think we should be whatever the best in us wants of us. That's true. We did our best.

"Brian Andrews, I hope you can rest in peace now," Buffy said to the moon. "We did our best. And we'll just keep on keeping on. We have to. It's our nature."

"And vampires must keep on, too," came a nearby voice. It was Viva, standing in the shadows, watching Buffy with glittery eyes. "It's our nature. You've done us both a favor, Slayer."

"I guess I did."

"But don't think I owe you anything."

"I don't."

"Don't think I won't kill you someday."

Buffy pulled out a stake and threw it at Viva. It caught her in the heart and she vanished in a whirlwind of ash.

"And don't think I won't either," Buffy said to the dust.

She turned to go into The Bronze. A tall, dark man stepped in front of her, blocking her way. She gasped, reached instinctively for her backpack, then smiled.

"Angel. Hi. What's up at the cave?"

"Bad things are coming our way. I'll tell you all about it."

Buffy put her arm through his, and her head on his shoulder. They left the noise of The Bronze for the still of the night.

And, hopefully, an hour or two of peace.

EPILOGUE

"**W**here are our patrons?" demanded Radello Gianakous of his daughter Allison, as he stood peering out the restaurant's front window. "If I remember correctly, we had business recently—lots of business, some kind of moony people, didn't we? Happy people, singing people—and we sold lots of food. I think we did, didn't we?"

Allison looked up at her Miss Sunnydale High trophy, now situated next to the crockery on the shelf over the wall. It wasn't Greek culture, but it looked really good. "I'm not sure we sold much food," she said to her father. "The pantry is still pretty well stocked up. But I bet we served a lot of water. There are tons of dirty water glasses in the kitchen."

Mr. Gianakous sighed heavily.

"Anyway," Allison said, turning from the window and tying on a bright, white apron, "we have a real cook now! Me! And just wait until you see the great dishes I'm going to prepare. I think we should have a grand opening all over again, start from scratch. What do you think?"

Radello sat down at the table in front of the naked Olympians. "Women aren't the best cooks," he said glumly. "In my family all the best chefs were men."

"It doesn't matter, Dad," said Allison. "Really. I want to do this, and you're going to let me. Aren't you?"

He scowled.

"I'm Miss Sunnydale," said Allison. "Mom would think that meant I had grown up."

Mr. Gianakous shrugged. Then he said, "Maybe I should pray for help. Maybe I should appeal to the old gods of our country to bring us help from above!"

Something inside Allison stirred, a vaguely uncomfortable sensation that made her catch her breath. "No, Dad," she said. "I think we'll do better on our own."

"Are you sure? I always liked the idea of powerful Mars, coming to aid the weak."

"Mars is Roman," said Allison. "Ares is Greek."

"Oh."

Allison took her father by the arm and led him back toward the kitchen. "Forget the gods. Why don't I show you what I've learned about cooking? It'll be fun. It'll be a father-daughter thing."

Radello stopped, tears in his eyes. "You are a wonderful, beautiful young woman. Your mother would be proud."

And instead of correcting her father, Allison only smiled, gave her dad a hug, and thought, *He's right. He's so right.*

About the Author

Elizabeth Massie is a two-time Bram Stoker Award winner who enjoys writing all kinds of fiction—horror, suspense, historicals, mainstream, even picture books for children. She is the author of several adult novels: *Sineater, Welcome Back To the Night,* and *Dark Shadows: Dreams of the Dark* (cowritten with Stephen Mark Rainey). Her work for young adults includes *The Great Chicago Fire, 1871* (available from Archway Paperbacks) and the upcoming series, *Young Founders.* For middle-grade readers, she has written the *Daughters of Liberty* trilogy (available from Minstrel Books). For the really little guys, she coauthored *Jambo, Watoto!* with her best friend and sister, Barbara Spilman Lawson. She has also written a number of third-grade readers for a major educational house. Elizabeth's short fiction has been published in a wide variety of magazines and anthologies, as well as in two collections of her work, *Southern Discomfort* and *Shadow Dreams. Rhymes and Reasons,* the 1990 PBS television special for which she wrote the teleplay, won a Parents' Choice Award.

ABOUT THE AUTHOR

Besides writing, Elizabeth's favorite things to do are reading, camping, hiking, and traveling. She lives in the Shenandoah Valley of Virginia, and is the mother of two wonderful young adults—Erin and Brian. In her spare time she performs in local theater (her most recent, and favorite, part was in *Little Shop of Horrors*—what a surprise!) and presents writers' workshops for both teachers and students.

Everyone's got his demons....

ANGEL™

If it takes an eternity, he will make amends.

Original stories based
on the TV show
Created by Joss Whedon
& David Greenwalt

Bullying.
Threats.
Bullets.

Locker searches? Metal detectors?

Fight back without fists.

fight for your rights:
take a stand against violence

BODY OF EVIDENCE
Thrillers starring Jenna Blake

"The first day at college, my professor dropped dead. The second day, I assisted at his autopsy. Let's hope I don't have to go through four years of this...."

When Jenna Blake starts her freshman year at Somerset University, it's an exciting time, filled with new faces and new challenges, not to mention parties and guys and...a job interview with the medical examiner that takes place in the middle of an autopsy! As Jenna starts her new job, she is drawn into a web of dangerous politics and deadly disease...a web that will bring her face-to-face with a pair of killers: one medical, and one all too human.

Body Bags
Thief of Hearts
Soul Survivor
Meets the Eye
Head Games
Skin Deep
Burning Bones
(Christopher Golden and Rick Hautala)

THREE NEW TITLES A YEAR

BY CHRISTOPHER GOLDEN

Bestselling coauthor of
Buffy the Vampire Slayer™: The Watcher's Guide

Buffy
the Vampire Slayer™

"Well, we could grind our
enemies into powder with a
sledgehammer, but gosh,
we did that last night."

—Xander

As long as there have been vampires,
there has been the Slayer. One girl
in all the world, to find them where
they gather and to stop the spread of
their evil and the swell of their numbers.

LOOK FOR A NEW TITLE
EVERY MONTH!

Based on the hit TV series created by
Joss Whedon